With her acclaimed, emotion-filled novels of love,
KAY HOOPER
has become a NATIONAL BESTSELLING AUTHOR,
a shining star among today's romance writers. . . .
Now, in an unforgettable tale of two unlikely lovers,
she finds true love can come when least expected
—and stay for a lifetime . . .

EYE OF THE BEHOLDER

"Good morning."

Tory gazed into his impossibly green eyes, thinking about the way she had acted last night. Had that wanton woman really been she? She felt heat suffuse her throat and steal up her face.

Devon chuckled. "Don't look so horrified; you'll hurt my feelings if you wake up every morning wearing that expression!"

"It's not that," she denied almost inaudibly. "It's just that I—that I've never—"

"You've never—?" he prompted softly.

"Felt that way before," she admitted.

"Neither have I."

She looked at him a little shyly. "No?"

"No." He traced the curve of her lips with a gentle finger. "Together we make magic, tough lady. . . ."

Praise for *The Matchmaker* by Kay Hooper:
"[An] overwhelming love story . . . filled with passion . . . outstanding!"

—*Rendezvous*

EYE OF THE BEHOLDER

KAY HOOPER

Originally published under the
pseudonym Kay Robbins.

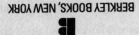

BERKLEY BOOKS, NEW YORK

Originally published under the pseudonym Kay Robbins.

EYE OF THE BEHOLDER

A Berkley Book / published by arrangement with the author

PRINTING HISTORY
Second Chance at Love edition published 1985
Berkley edition / March 1994

ISBN: 0-425-14127-6

BERKLEY®
Berkley Books are published by The Berkley Publishing Group, 200 Madison Avenue, New York, New York 10016. BERKLEY and the "B" design are trademarks belonging to Berkley Publishing Corporation.

PRINTED IN THE UNITED STATES OF AMERICA

10 9 8 7 6 5 4 3 2 1

To Leslie, my editor,
for her patience, understanding, and ability.
And for being my camera's lens
to focus what I see.

"That I should love a bright, particular star
And think to wed it."

—William Shakespeare
All's Well That Ends Well

EYE OF THE BEHOLDER

Chapter 1

"MARRY ME, ANGEL, and I'll take you to faraway places!"

Tory stared blankly at the man standing on her front porch. He was leaning against the doorframe and staring off into the blue fall sky, showing her an admittedly handsome profile. He was roughly six feet tall, a copper-redhead with astonishingly bright green eyes, dressed in neat dark slacks, a cream-colored shirt open at the throat, and a gold sports jacket, and he looked to be in his mid-thirties.

And she'd never seen him before in her life.

It was just what she needed to cap off a truly distressing morning. With a detachment born of lack of sleep, she considered her appearance and decided that if the stranger would only look at her, he'd probably run screaming. She was wearing her old plaid bathrobe, which was badly tattered about the hem, ragged slippers, which made her feet look twice their actual size, and a towel wrapped turbanlike around her wet hair. And in her left hand, she clutched a percolator, cord trailing.

"I'd marry Attila the Hun if he'd only find my coffee," she told the stranger finally.

The man straightened in a hurry and stared down at her. "Who the hell are you?" he asked comically.

"Tory," she answered politely.

"Where's Angela?" he demanded.

"If you're referring to the lady who used to live here—and I gather you are—she doesn't anymore. Sorry to be the one to break it to you, but she's on her honeymoon. In Bermuda, I think."

"How could they get married without me?" he exclaimed, clearly aggrieved.

"It only takes two, you know. One to be the bride and one to be the groom."

"And one to be the best man," he added. "Dammit, why didn't they let me know?"

"I couldn't say."

He blinked, apparently seeing the percolator for the first time. "Coffee? Thanks, I'd love some."

Tory gave way automatically as he stepped into the house. She toyed mildly with the idea of calling the police, but the phone wasn't connected yet, and besides, the man seemed harmless. Sighing, she closed the door.

He was halfway to the kitchen by then, obviously familiar with the house. He made his way through the confusion of boxes and crates yet to be unpacked, still talking in that ridiculously aggrieved voice and apparently unconcerned that his listener was a total stranger.

"They could have reached me if they'd tried. I mean, I was only out in the desert; I wasn't on the moon. Was it my fault the sheikh decided he wanted another airplane and the ambassador was having kittens? Was it my fault everyone seemed to want to leave the Middle East on the same day and I had to bum a ride with an Air Force transport on a milk run? Was it my fault the last stop was D.C. and everybody wanted to leave *there* on the same day and I had to borrow Bobby's plane? Well? *Was* it my fault?"

Appealed to directly for the first time, Tory blinked and tried to absorb his confusing conversation. "Um . . . no. No, of course it wasn't your fault. Who could ever think it was your fault?" She gestured, only then realizing that she was still clutching the percolator.

"I can't make coffee without the pot. Here." He took the percolator and began filling it with water, adding darkly, "Phillip will blame me, if I know him."

"Phillip?" Tory made a determined effort to think. "Isn't that Angela's new husband?"

"And my brother." His hand dived into the nearest box and produced the coffee like a magician's rabbit. "Ah. Now you have to marry me; I've found your coffee."

"You weren't proposing to me," she reminded him, beginning to be amused by his leapfrog conversation.

"Well, I am now. Marry me?"

"No, thank you. I make it a habit never to marry men I don't know." Tory leaned against the counter and watched him spoon coffee into the pot with undiminished good humor. "Did you have a habit of proposing to your brother's fiancée, or was today a red-letter day?" she asked dryly.

"Oh, it was a habit. Started the day we met, actually. I told Angela that if Phillip hadn't caught her first, I'd propose. She told me not to let that stop me, so I proposed. She turned me down but said that it'd be good practice for me. So I kept proposing. I've come up with some pretty creative proposals," he finished in a self-congratulatory tone.

"I'm sure. Um . . . putting it as delicately as possible, didn't your brother object to all this proposing?"

"Of course not. Angela wouldn't leave him. He did say once that if I threw Angela across my saddle and galloped off into the night, he'd hunt me down like a mad dog. A gentleman's warning, you know."

"Uh-huh." Tory forced her mind into a higher gear; she was working toward full throttle but, at this rate, never hoped to get there. It did occur to her, however, that she was taking this uninvited guest with surprising calm. Probably lack of sleep. "If you're Phillip's brother," she said, "then your name is York."

"Devon York. And you're Tory—?"

"Michaels."

"So now we know who we are. What color is your hair?"

She was watching him unwrap coffee cups—and where on earth had he found them? His question sank in. "My hair?"

"All I can see is a purple towel," he explained apologetically.

"Purple?" Tory knew she sounded like an idiot, but she was trying to remember the events of an extremely confusing morning. She'd reached for the box of towels and grabbed the one on top—had it been purple?

"Black?" he guessed.

"What? Oh . . . yes, black." It set up a train of thought. "Your brother's dark," she said suddenly.

"Yes, he is. So's my sister. There was a redheaded Scotsman somewhere in the past, and occasionally he turns up and flaunts his genes. A throwback, I think they call it. I'm a throwback. Are your eyes gray or green?"

"Gray, usually," she answered in an absent tone, mentally conjuring an image of the tall, dark Phillip York and the merry, brunette Angela. They had certainly seemed devoted to each other, she remembered. Flaunts his jeans? No . . . surely he'd said *genes*. What on earth was wrong with her?

"How old are you?"

"Twenty-sev—" Abruptly, he had her full attention. "What's with the third degree?"

"Well, I'm drinking your coffee."

"Not yet, and so what?"

"I like to know a little about a woman when I drink her coffee and propose to her."

"Oh." For the life of her, Tory didn't know how to respond to that. She decided to let it pass.

He grinned suddenly, and the charm of that did something odd to her ability to breathe with normal ease. A little voice in her head announced mournfully that she really shouldn't have answered the doorbell.

"You're not with it this morning, are you?" he asked cheerfully.

Tory stared at him. The sense of ill-use that had grown steadily all morning abruptly overwhelmed her, and she forgot that she was talking to a stranger. She began her little tale of woe slowly and steadily, but her voice increased its speed and lost some of its control by the end.

"I slept on a mattress on the floor last night, because when I got here—at midnight—I discovered that the movers hadn't put the bed up, and I didn't have a single tool to put it up myself. And my alarm clock, which was in the box right beside the mattress, went off at seven o'clock this morning. I fell off the mattress and nearly had a nervous breakdown, because the first night in a strange house is terrible, and then I tripped on the sheet getting up and fell into a box of books. By the time I turned off the damn clock, I wasn't about to go back to sleep, so I decided to take a shower. I didn't turn the water on until I got in; it was freezing, and I hate cold showers. When I got out, I couldn't find the towels for ten minutes, so I've probably caught pneumonia. And all my clothes were packed in sealed boxes except for this robe. My hair dryer short-circuited. The only slippers I could find were these—"

"Very fetching."

"—things. I nearly broke my neck on the stairs. I got lost trying to find the kitchen, and I was viciously attacked by the door to the basement. None of the light switches were where they were supposed to be, and it's *dark* at the crack of dawn. It took me twenty minutes to find the percolator, and I couldn't find my coffee!"

Her voice rose on the last word, the sound that of human tolerance pushed way past its limit. She took a deep breath, viewing his twitching lips and laughing eyes with real dislike. "No, I'm not with it this morning, Mr. York."

"Devon," he insisted politely.

She ignored that. "I'm so not with it that I let a stranger—obviously spending the odd day away from the asylum—come into my house, tell me strange tales about proposing to his almost-sister-in-law, arguing with sheikhs and ambassadors in deserts, bumming rides with transport planes, and borrowing other planes, and—and I let him make *coffee!*"

"I think you need a cup," he murmured, clearly trying not to laugh.

"There's no milk," she told him miserably, this last grievance threatening to overpower all the rest. "I hate black coffee."

"We'll work something out." He thrust a white handkerchief into her hand. "Take this."

Tory wiped her eyes and glared at him. "I don't cry," she announced coldly.

"Of course not."

"Don't patronize me, dammit!"

"I wasn't. Look, we can handle this one of two ways."

She wondered vaguely what they were supposed

to be handling but felt too utterly limp to ask.

"Either you can borrow my shoulder, which I'm told is rather good at absorbing the woes and cares of everyday life, or else you can sit down and put your feet up while I fix a much-needed breakfast for both of us."

"Can you cook?" Tory asked, feeling a faint flicker of interest.

"Certainly I can cook."

"Oh." She hiccuped and glared at him as though it were his fault. "Well, I don't want your shoulder," she announced defiantly.

"I'm crushed. Hold on a second." He disappeared in the general direction of the living room, appearing a moment later with a low-armed, high-backed chair that had been stuffed for comfort and covered in brushed velvet. He had one of her colorful throw pillows under an arm.

"You don't have very much furniture," he noted.

"I've never had a house before." She watched him position the chair in one corner of the large kitchen. "That doesn't belong in here."

"We'll put it back when we're finished. Now, have a seat."

Tory decided not to waste a glare. She sat down in the chair, tugging at the lapels of her robe as it suddenly occurred to her that only a frayed belt kept it in place and that she wore absolutely nothing underneath it.

Devon drew forward a sealed box marked BOOKS, placed the pillow on top of it, then wordlessly grasped her ankles and lifted them onto the pillow.

"I can do that," she muttered, alarmed at the breathless sound of her own voice.

"My pleasure," he said solemnly. Then he turned away and began searching through the various boxes piled in the room, finding what he needed seemingly by magic.

Tory wondered if she should protest his cheerful search through her belongings, but she couldn't bring herself to, somehow. It was quite a change for her to be taken care of like this, and she wasn't sure it was a good thing. Especially since she was aware that his offer of a shoulder to cry on had tempted her—very much.

And that was unnerving. Granted, she'd had a rough morning, and the preceding few weeks had been far from easy. But she was still annoyed by the weakness of tears. Because what she'd told Devon was true: She didn't cry. Not on the outside, anyway. Not where everyone could see. And she was a very capable, reasonable, efficient woman. Everyone said so. Even though, she thought with mild irritation, "everyone" always qualified the statement by adding the rider, "for an artist, that is."

"Will this do in place of milk?"

She looked up hastily to see that he was holding several small packets of powdered creamer. She wondered, with a vague sense of annoyance, where he had gotten them and if he was the type of man who'd taken the Boy Scouts' motto of "Be prepared" for his own. Such efficiency was grating, particularly after her chaotic morning.

"I'll settle for it," she answered rather ungraciously.

"Great." He didn't, she noted, seem the slightest bit upset by her tone. He merely poured a cup of coffee, politely asked how she liked it, then handed her the cup.

"So you just arrived last night?" he questioned chattily.

"Mm." Tory was sipping the reviving coffee and watching him reposition boxes to clear space for cooking.

"From where?"

"Arizona," Tory replied, beginning to understand his verbal shorthand.

"Beautiful country out there," he offered.

"Yes."

"Why'd you leave? Or am I being nosy?"

Tory started to tell him that she'd left the West because she'd grown bored with deserts as subjects, but she answered his second question instead. "Of course you're being nosy; it seems to be a character flaw."

Devon accepted the observation philosophically. "Looks that way, doesn't it?" Before she could reply, he was going on cheerfully. "What d'you think of West Virginia?"

Reflecting silently that this man's bump of curiosity was a large one, Tory answered resignedly. "It's beautiful. I love mountains."

"So do I. Scrambled, fried, poached, or boiled?"

Tory blinked at the egg he was tossing lightly from

hand to hand. "Um . . . scrambled, I guess."

"Good. No matter what I try, they always end up scrambled."

"Then why did you ask?"

"Good manners."

Sighing, Tory took another sip of coffee and forced her reluctant mind into the next highest gear. She crossed her ankles and watched him moving about the kitchen. Interest stirred to life inside her, and Tory told herself that it was entirely professional. Her instinctive eye for form, color, and movement was attracted by his unconscious grace and by the clean, masculine lines of his lean body.

Shunting the thoughts aside, Tory fiercely pulled her gaze away from him and stared down at her coffee. Uh-uh! Never again! Two years of painting deserts had done a lot to heal wounds, but she wasn't about to risk her hard-won peace by attempting another portrait—especially not a portrait of a man.

Rushing into speech to occupy her wayward mind, Tory said, "Let's have your vital statistics. Fair trade."

"Okay," he responded genially. "What d'you want to know?"

Tory lifted her cup in a whatever-you-like gesture.

Devon turned the bacon strips over and then began to break eggs into a mixing bowl. "Let's see, then . . . Height, weight, serial number?"

"Cute," she murmured.

"In no mood for humor, I see."

"If you can ask that after hearing about my morning—"

"Sorry." He looked thoughtful for a moment and

then, responding to her inquiring look, said gravely, "I'm trying to think of something really exciting to tell you so you'll say yes the next time I propose. Maybe if I likened myself to James Bond?"

"Not my type."

"Ummm, Horatio Hornblower?"

"I'd get seasick."

"The Scarlet Pimpernel?"

"Sorry."

"Heathcliff?"

"Too brooding."

"Don Quixote?"

Tory stared at him over the rim of her cup. "This is all very revealing, you know. Either you watch a lot of old movies or else you read a lot of books."

He grinned. "Both."

"Uh-huh. Look, why don't you just tell me who *you* are, and never mind the heroes of fiction."

"If you insist."

"I do."

"Remember that phrase; you'll have need of it later."

Tory blinked; it took her a moment to realize he was referring to something along the lines of "Do you take this man." She sighed. "Tell me about yourself before I start to think you're just an apparition in my nightmarish morning."

"Thanks a lot."

"You asked for it."

"I suppose. Okay, then. I'm thirty-two years old, single, reasonably well off. I can eat almost anything, never hog the blankets at night, and don't object to taking out the garbage. I can make beds, I never drop my socks on the floor, and I'm not addicted to televised sports. As you see, I can cook, and I don't expect to be waited on. I'm also a dandy dishwasher. In fact"—he gave her a grin that was comical in its pleased surprise—"I'm perfect husband material."

Tory, elbow propped on the low arm of her chair and chin in hand, stared at him. Gravely, she asked, "Then why on earth are you still running around loose?"

"I don't know," he told her seriously. "I suppose because no woman has yet appreciated my sterling qualities."

"Those weren't quite the vital statistics I had in mind."

"Just thought I'd make my pitch, you know."

"It was wasted on me, I'm afraid."

"Determinedly single?" he queried with a lifted brow.

"Something like that."

"I'll have to see what I can do about that."

"Don't bother." Before he could respond, she asked casually, "What do you do for a living? You didn't say."

He looked wounded. "I have to leave something to the imagination. For the chase, you understand. Mystery."

Tory thought about that. "Who's chasing whom?" she asked politely.

"I'm chasing you," he told her cordially.

Chapter **2**

TORY GAZED AT HIM, thoughtful, considering. Any man, she decided finally, who could say what he'd just said to a woman who looked as if she'd just been dragged by an ear through a hurricane was obviously a mental case. Accordingly, she humored him.

"I refuse to be chased on an empty stomach," she said mildly.

"Well, we'll fix that," he told her cheerfully, and he proceeded to finish preparing breakfast.

They ate the meal on a table made of boxes, since Tory had yet to acquire a kitchen table, and Devon York continued his questioning and more or less one-sided dialogue.

"Do you like animals?"

"Yes."

"Have any pets?"

15

"No."

"What's your sign?"

"You've got to be kidding."

"Well, these one-word answers of yours aren't very forthcoming, you know. What's your sign?"

"Taurus."

"No wonder you're answering in monosyllables."

"I beg your pardon?"

"Taureans are like that. Tranquil, serene. And fond of one-word answers." He studied her thoughtfully. "In fact, I'm surprised you cut loose a little while ago; your morning must have *really* been lousy."

"It was."

He grinned a little. "But you're back on balance now."

Tory pushed her empty plate away and leaned back, sipping her second cup of coffee and beginning to feel more human. "I'm getting there," she told him wryly. "And what's *your* sign?"

"Sagittarius," he replied cheerfully.

She filed the information away in her mind, although she didn't quite know why. "What are Sagittarians noted for?"

"Their charm." Devon got up and carried their plates to the sink.

Ruefully, she said, "You obviously don't believe in hiding your light under a bushel."

He was running water into the sink and efficiently dealing with the after-meal cleanup. "'Course not. Faint heart never won fair lady . . . or something like that."

"Oh, are we back to that?"

"We never left it, fair lady."

Tory sighed. She watched him roll up the sleeves of his shirt—he'd tossed the jacket over a box some time before—and plunge his hands into the sudsy water. Idly, she wondered how she'd pose him, then hastily discarded the speculation. But her fingers were itching to pick up charcoal or pencil and begin a preliminary sketch...

"You're staring at me," he noted, sending her a sideways glance.

"Just looking for the heart on your sleeve," she explained dryly.

He smiled modestly. "Love and a cough can't be hidden."

"You're a nut."

"I've been called worse."

"Doubtless by someone who knew you well."

"Ouch." He chuckled softly. "With one-word answers and one-liners, you're obviously tops."

"Practice," Tory heard herself say and, as if that wasn't enough, heard herself add, "with a man sharp enough to cut himself." She managed to end the admission on a note of absolute finality, irritated by her mind's refusal to let go of a painful memory.

She had looked away from Devon, and as she glanced back she encountered a suddenly keen, searching look from the vivid green eyes. The unexpectedness of it threw her for a moment, but then Tory hastily revised her impressions of Devon York. Obviously, she realized, here was yet a second man who was sharp enough to cut himself, and she felt wariness slipping into her mind.

Devon spoke quickly, the flash of shrewdness gone from his eyes as though it had never existed. In its place was the good humor of a moment before. "I sharpen my wits on dumb animals," he said solemnly. "That way I can convince myself I'm quicker than I really am."

The absurdity caught Tory before she could fully erect a wary mask, and she heard herself give a startled giggle.

He looked ridiculously gratified. Bowing from the waist with a certain style, he flourished a dishcloth and said sonorously, "Marry me, I beg of you," and added gravely, "I need that giggle; you're a terrific audience."

Tory stared at him for a moment, then looked to the ceiling for inspiration. "I don't know where we are, Toto," she murmured plaintively, "but it isn't Kansas."

"You didn't answer me," he reproved.

"Wanta bet?"

He looked hurt.

Tory relented and said mildly, "All right then. I'll marry you when it snows in Miami on the Fourth of July."

Devon leaned back against the counter and appeared thoughtful. "That's a very creative refusal," he said finally.

"I thought you'd appreciate it."

He rubbed the bridge of his nose reflectively. "I

get the feeling," he said, "that this is going to turn into quite a contest."

Tory felt a sudden foreboding. What had she begun by allowing Devon York into her house? "Don't you have to get back to your desert?" she asked carefully.

He smiled. "No."

"Your job?"

"I'm flexible."

"You are *not,*" she said strongly, "going to turn me into a vacation hobby! Audience or no audience!"

"I wouldn't think of it," he responded soulfully.

Tory stared at him suspiciously. "I don't believe you."

"O ye of little faith."

Curtly, she said, "I don't know you well enough to have faith—just well enough to be worried."

"Thanks a lot."

"Mr. York—"

"Please. I thought we'd at least gotten past that."

Tory looked at him, at the odd grin that did something to her breathing, and her unease grew even as she held firmly to a level voice. "Devon, then—"

"Thank you," he murmured.

She ignored the gentle irony. "You may have a flexible job, but I have quite a few things to do. I have to unpack and get the house in order, and then I have to go back to work."

"What d'you do?" he asked interestedly.

"I paint," she said after a moment, flatly.

He looked at her. "Really? What d'you paint?"

Tory was uncomfortably aware that there had been

a second flash of shrewdness in his remarkable eyes. "Mostly landscapes and still lifes."

Devon snapped his fingers in sudden realization. "Most of those crates in there hold canvases, don't they?" he asked, nodding toward the den.

"Yes."

"You're prolific," he guessed.

Tory shrugged. "Active," she qualified.

He abandoned the subject abruptly. "Well, you'll need help unpacking," he said cheerfully.

"No—" Tory began hastily, only to be interrupted.

"I can set up your bed and help move furniture, and I'm first-rate at carrying boxes and hanging pictures. The yard needs some work, and there's that leaking pipe in the basement, too. Phillip has a house nearer town; I can use my key and borrow his lawnmower and some tools—"

"Hold it!" Tory took a deep breath and fought down a sudden, inexplicable panic. She stared at this tall, maddeningly efficient stranger and wondered wildly if he'd decided to put down roots here. "Look, I appreciate the—the offer. Really. But I'm accustomed to taking care of myself. I *like* taking care of myself."

"That was before I came along," he said reasonably.

Tory struggled with herself. "I don't need your help," she said evenly.

He looked dismayed, and for the life of her, Tory didn't know if his expression was real or sham. "I wish you'd let me help," he said unhappily. "I'm at loose ends for a while, and with Phillip and Angela away I don't know a soul around here."

Tory felt herself weakening. She *knew* she was weakening yet couldn't seem to stop herself. It was that little grin of his, she decided irritably. It was a fallen-angel grin, a beguiling combination of charm, uncertainty, mischief, and defiance. *There's one born every minute!* she reminded herself ruefully, thinking that P. T. Barnum was a wise man.

"I can help?" Devon ventured hopefully, obviously taking note of the defeated gesture she'd made almost unconsciously.

She glared at him and muttered, "Why not."

"Terrific. Is it Victoria?"

"What?" she asked, completely at sea.

"Your name. Is it short for Victoria?"

"No."

"That's interesting."

Tory rubbed at a vague sort of ache between her eyes. "Look. Could you do me a favor?"

"Just ask."

"Leave."

Devon looked hurt.

Sighing, Tory said, "I can't deal with you this morning. Any other morning, I could probably make a stab at it. But not *this* morning."

He appeared to think it over, then demanded suspiciously, "Can I come back for lunch?"

Tory stared at him for a long moment. "If you bring it or cook it yourself," she said finally in a severely put-upon tone.

Devon lifted an eyebrow at her. "Thank you for

that gracious invitation."

"You're welcome. Thank you for breakfast. Good-bye."

With undiminished cheerfulness, Devon rolled down his sleeves, donned his jacket, and left, begging her politely not to get up on his account.

Tory sat there for long moments, a half-empty coffee cup in her hand. An absentminded swallow collided with giggles and caused a coughing fit, bringing relative sobriety. She rose to her feet and set the cup on the counter, thinking that she'd really better stop enjoying Devon York's company. It could get addictive. And since she'd twice seen evidence of an extremely sharp man beneath the genial facade, she thought that being addicted to Devon York's company could be a dangerous thing indeed.

When the doorbell rang at eleven that morning, Tory went to see if Devon had returned. No one else would visit her in this part of the country. But it wasn't Devon.

It was, instead, a delivery man bearing the most tremendous basket of long-stemmed red roses—bridal roses, she noted—that Tory had ever seen in her life. Bemused, she carried the huge basket into the living room and set it on a low table beside the French doors opening onto the patio. She made two discoveries then: one, that the flowers were scented silk; and, two, that there was a card.

The card was handwritten in a firm, curiously exact, block-printed style, undeniably masculine and shrieking of a logical, clear-thinking man of purpose. Tory had studied various theories regarding handwriting some years before out of curiosity and as a sort of offshoot of her artistic work. She had found the science fascinating and now automatically studied the handwriting before actually reading the words.

And she knew that if she had studied this handwriting knowing nothing about the man it represented, she would never have pictured Devon York as that man. This writing, she decided, belonged to a man who was sharply intelligent, extremely well educated, concise, practical, and logical. Each stroke of pen revealed self-confidence, assurance, pride bordering on arrogance, exactitude, unerring logic, mathematical precision, and utter and complete self-control.

There was, in fact, little to remind her of the affable man who had cheerfully cooked breakfast for her that morning. No creative whimsy, no subtlety, no radical sense of humor—and *no* uncertainty.

Tory frowned and, almost as an afterthought, read the message. It was a quotation from Donne, and it represented a drastic contrast between what was written—and *how* it was written:

Whoever loves, if he do not propose
The right true end of love, he's one that goes
To sea for nothing but to make him sick.

Wandering over to her brick fireplace, Tory propped the card up on the mantel and stared at it musingly. Then she looked beside the card at the mirror above the mantel, and at the reflection there.

She saw a woman whose black hair fell in a long, loose pageboy and gleamed with blue highlights, framing a face that was irritatingly heart-shaped and tanned a golden brown. Out of that face shone eyes that were usually gray but sometimes green or blue or violet or hazel, and that always looked too large for the face they occupied. The nose was a snubbed affair, turning up at the end and perfectly suited for the face even if its owner despised it. High, flat cheekbones were a gift from a Romany ancestor, the same one who had bequeathed her the raven hair and a tendency toward introspection.

Tory knew, in fact, that she was almost a mirror replica of her paternal great-great-grandmother, who had been a Gypsy. An oil painting of her was still packed in its crate, waiting to be hung. Tory treasured the portrait because she had always felt such an affinity for the woman it represented.

Pushing Great-Great-Grandmother Magda from her mind, Tory continued her thoughtful scrutiny of herself. She was enough of an artist to know that her face was striking, enough of a woman to wish certain changes had been made.

Still, she thought with some satisfaction that Devon would be surprised when he saw her; the bedraggled, shell-shocked creature of this morning bore little resemblance to the woman now reflected in the mirror. Tory was not, she well knew, a woman who looked her best upon waking. The morning saw a bleary-eyed, pale face with no animation and no pretensions whatsoever to beauty. Only after coffee, a shower, and an interlude of walking about and waking up thoroughly did Tory feel human. And look it.

It was a highly vexing trait for one who had spent her life trying to disprove the popular theory that artists were vague, untidy creatures, irrational in mood and careless in habit. Tory prided herself on her logic and dedication to a profession she'd inherited a talent for, and on her rational approach to that profession.

Backing away from the hearth a few steps, she studied the rest of Tory Michaels as revealed by the tilted mirror. Too thin, she decided critically. Almost fragile, dammit. And the ribbed turtleneck sweater made of a soft, clinging gray wool only highlighted that unwelcome fragility.

Not surprising, all things considered, she thought. Working hard in desert heat and being one who never worried much about meals, she was bound to have lost a little weight. Still, she was hardly fragile, appearance notwithstanding. Tough. That was it.

She smoothed her palms down her jean-clad thighs and thought back to the childhood days when her father had called her a gazelle because of her long legs and habit of always rushing about. She'd never really grown into the legs, she thought a bit sadly. The early prediction of height had not materialized; she was only a little over five feet tall. And she never rushed these days; that meant wasted energy and was hardly efficient.

Tory sighed and stepped back to the hearth, returning to her study of Devon's card. It wasn't signed, but it was his, she knew. And she knew that the safest thing for her to do would be to lock all her doors and refuse to set eyes on the man again. Because if this card and her interpretation of it were to be trusted, he would have to be the most complex man she'd ever encountered.

She wasn't given to armchair analysis, but Tory trusted her impressions of people. Hers was a rational process of analysis, based on years of studying human beings and colored only slightly by what she studiously avoided terming "artistic intuition." And she had been wrong only once—when she'd allowed her emotions to influence her judgment.

Biting her lip, she turned away from the card and the puzzle-man it represented, returning to her unpacking. Clearing her mind, she carefully unwrapped a very old and delicate vase. It was, like Great-Great-Grandmother Magda's portrait, a part of her heritage. Tory sat cross-legged on the floor amid packing straw and wrapping paper, holding the vase and gazing down at it.

"Hello?"

Tory looked up swiftly, immediately recognizing the deep voice. "I thought you had good manners!" she accused.

"I rang the bell," Devon told her firmly. "You didn't hear it, I guess."

Getting up, she carried the vase over to the mantel and placed it carefully near one end. "I guess," she retorted, suspicion heavy in her voice as she turned around to face him. He was looking her up and down, and Tory was both pleased and irked by the surprise in his vivid green eyes.

"I knew there'd be an improvement," he said, "but I never expected an entirely new woman."

"Thank you!" she snapped before seeing the laugh in his eyes.

"You are a lovely woman, Tory Michaels," he said seriously, the laugh still present, but different.

"Um . . . thank you," she said again, uncertainly this time. Tory decided she really didn't want to consider how his expression had subtly changed; along that path lay the danger she sensed from this man. "I assume the flowers were from you," she said rather hastily. "They're beautiful. But why silk? That's an expensive gesture."

Devon had wandered over to the fireplace and was gazing at the vase she'd just placed there. "Ming," he noted almost absently.

"Why silk?" Tory repeated, disregarding his obvious knowledge of porcelain.

He looked down at her. "Because they last."

"Oh."

Devon gestured toward the card propped on the mantel. "What'd you think of that?"

"You mean your poetic turn of mind?"

"I mean my proposal," he corrected.

"You'd better get pills for seasickness."

He chuckled softly. "You think I'm going to sea for only that reason?"

"I think it'll be the only result of your trip."

"Well, I'm a good sailor. I'll take my chances."

Tory abruptly decided that their metaphorical little "trip" had gone on long enough. She turned and threaded her way among the boxes and crates, intent on completing the task at hand. "Are you sure you don't have to get back to your desert?" she asked over her shoulder.

"Positive. I can help you with this—Oh, wait a minute!"

With that disjointed utterance, he abruptly went out into the foyer, returning seconds later with a rather large box, brightly wrapped and tied with a big red bow, which he handed to Tory.

She felt the box shift in her hands and stared at the small holes—air holes, she realized warily—in the sides. "What's this?"

"A present. Open it."

Tory sat down on a large crate, the box resting carefully on her knees, and gazed up at him. "Will something jump out at me?"

"Probably."

"Devon—"

"Open it."

Cautiously, Tory slid the ribbons and bow off the box and even more cautiously lifted the lid. Then she began to laugh softly. "He's adorable!"

"He" was a red-yellow tabby kitten with huge brilliant green eyes and remarkably large pointed ears. Around his neck hung a somewhat bedraggled red bow, bearing obvious marks of curious little teeth. And he immediately left the box to cling to Tory's sweater and hide his face beneath her long hair. His purr was a startlingly bass rumble.

"Where'd you get him?" Tory asked, then added, "Him?"

"Him," Devon confirmed, grinning down at her. "And I got him from one of Phillip's neighbors. I've met her—Mrs. Jenkins—before; she breeds cats as a business. Anyway, she saw me loading tools and things and came over to ask if I knew anyone who might want a kitten. Of course, right away I thought of you—"

"Of course."

"—and I said sure. As soon as I saw this little fellow, I knew he was the one. And he was cheap." Devon started to laugh. "It seems that one of Mrs. Jenkins's prize-winning Abyssinians escaped the cattery and fell in with a ne'er-do-well tom whose only claim to royal blood was a possible smattering of Siamese. Mrs. Jenkins deduced that from the ensuing noise. Anyway, this little guy's the sole result of that memorable night. What'll you name him?"

"Oh, he'll name himself. Cats always do." Tory looked up at the man who was fast becoming less of a stranger. "Thank you, Devon."

Shrugging slightly, Devon said, "A house isn't a home until a cat's lived in it."

"Is that a proverb?"

"If it isn't, it should be." In the magical way that by now seemed customary, he produced a small carton of milk. "I've got some more stuff out in the truck— cat food, a litter box, and litter. I'll go get it."

Tory stood as he left the room, crossing to the

window and pulling aside the drapes Angela had left, gazing out. "Truck?" she wondered aloud to her new houseguest. The answer was parked in her driveway, just behind her own gray Cougar; it was a four-wheel-drive pickup truck with a roll bar and a brilliantly swirling "sunset" paint job. A sense of familiarity crystallized as Tory realized it was Phillip York's truck.

She carried the kitten into the kitchen and poured some milk into a saucer, setting the kitten down to enjoy his first meal in his new home. Devon came in bearing cat food, which he placed on the counter, and a litter box and bag of litter.

"Where d'you want his box?"

Gesturing toward a small room off the kitchen, she said, "In the storage room, I guess."

Rapidly finishing off his milk, the kitten decided to explore and made a beeline for the living room and the fascinating clutter of boxes and packing materials expressly designed to provide hours of enjoyment for felines. Tory followed, fascinated by the kitten's fascination.

It occurred to her somewhat belatedly that although this second visit of Devon's had found her aware, alert, and awake, she had accepted his presence with the same curiously detached bemusement that had held her in its grip this morning.

It was an unnerving thought.

She discovered a new addition to the living room at that moment: a picnic basket. It was a large wicker affair, clearly designed to hold enough food for an army.

"Lunch," Devon explained, coming into the room and obviously following her gaze. "You told me to either bring it or cook it myself, remember?"

"So I did."

"Want to eat now or wait awhile?"

"Whenever you like."

"Now, then. I'm hungry."

Tory felt unnerved again, because she was becoming entirely too companionable with this man. "You're an insidious man!" she accused suddenly.

Devon, busily clearing a space in the middle of the living room floor, looked up at her with limpid eyes. "Which definition are you thinking of?" he asked, his voice soft. "Something spreading harm in a subtle manner? Or something beguiling and seductive?"

Tory couldn't think of a single damn thing to say in response to that. But she answered his question silently: *beguiling and seductive!*

"Well?"

She made a major production out of fishing the kitten from a crate filled with packing straw. "I should show him where his box is."

"You're stalling, Tory."

For some odd reason, it seemed as if she'd never heard her name spoken aloud before. She felt a mask beginning to grip her face. Guarded. Defensive. Wary.

"Actually," Devon said gravely, "I think *insidious* was the wrong word entirely. *Stubborn,* maybe. Or *helpful.* I like *helpful.* I like *being* helpful."

Tory didn't know whether to laugh or hit him with something. She sighed instead. "I'm going to show my new houseguest where his box is."

"You do that. I'll have this stuff ready when you get back."

She headed for the storage room. Several things occurred to her in the moments granted for reflection. She wasn't quite sure which man Devon York actually was: the genial, whimsical man . . . or the man who had looked up at her for a timeless moment with a shocking intensity in his vivid green eyes.

And she wasn't quite sure which she feared the most.

But what she was sure of was the fact that he meant to be a part of her life for at least a while. And, deny it though she would, she was tired of being alone.

Chapter **3**

IT WAS THE GENIAL, whimsical man who offered companionship during a curious little picnic in the middle of her living room floor; the brief flash of intensity in his green eyes might have been purely her imagination. Tory responded to him as calmly and as bemusedly as she had all morning, but a part of her perception was occupied in trying to probe beneath the facade he wore as easily as a second skin.

She knew that his straightforward good humor *was* a facade, or rather she sensed that it was. Although maybe his intensity was a natural part of him, a glimpse of brief, dazzling whiteness from one of a diamond's many facets. Whatever that hint of complexity was, it disturbed her—because it also intrigued her.

And she had no business being intrigued by Devon York. His very presence injected uncertainty into her life, stealing control from her and knocking her off the balance she'd achieved. He seemed to possess the uncanny ability to draw her emotions closer to the surface and away from her own guiding hand.

It bothered her. Badly.

"Earth to Tory?"

She blinked and hastily recalled her wandering attention. *Damn!* "Sorry," she murmured. "You were saying?"

"Asking, actually." His green eyes were unreadable for an instant before resuming their clear cheerfulness. "Are you a famous sort of artist?"

Tory almost laughed but managed not to. She was beginning to realize that Devon was, if nothing else, a peculiar kind of man; he could say or ask something in the most outrageous terms and yet sound perfectly grave. "No," she answered dryly, "I'm not a famous sort of artist. Art isn't the field to get into if one's after fame; Picassos aren't born every day."

"Ah." Momentarily distracted, Devon leaned sideways to fish the curious kitten out of the wicker hamper, where the remains of lunch reposed. He was spat at for his trouble, and placatingly gave the kitten a piece of drumstick to chew on.

Watching tiny feline teeth gnawing ferociously, Tory said, "Keep an eye on him so he doesn't get any bones; they could hurt him."

Devon nodded and stretched long legs out in front of him; they were both sitting on a gaily checkered tablecloth spread on the floor, backs against stout packing crates. He returned to the subject of art and fame. "I wondered. Your name's familiar, and for some reason I associate it with art."

"Jeremy Michaels."

Devon frowned only for a moment. "Now I've got it. And how could I forget! The experts have called him America's answer to Michelangelo; what he could express in sculpture has never been surpassed, before or since, by any other American artist—and by few in history. And he was also considered an expert in detecting forgeries in all forms of art; museums and collectors the world over trusted him to authenticate artworks." Devon looked at her steadily, questioningly. "And he was—?"

"My father." Tory smiled faintly. "So you see, I've been familiar with fame secondhand all my life. I don't care to experience it firsthand."

"*Because* your father was famous?"

"Maybe." She stared off into memory. "He told me once that fame was damnably easy to acquire—and damnably hard to control. But he did it." She smiled again. "Daddy's bathroom was completely mirrored. Not out of vanity, but out of humility. He said that after he'd stumble in there each morning and see the reflections of himself, unshaven, red-eyed, and wearing baggy pajamas, he never had to be reminded that he was . . . just a man."

Devon was watching her, not with the intensity she half dreaded, but with a curious *intentness*. "Did he expect you to follow in his footsteps and sculpt? Or did you feel that you had to paint to be different from him?"

"Neither." Tory was responding more to compelling green eyes than to his questions, and that bewildered her. "Daddy never pressured me. In fact, he gave me a lot of good reasons to avoid art altogether. I think he was pleased when I decided to paint, but I also think he would have been just as pleased if I'd chosen to paint houses instead of canvases. As long as I was happy with my decision, so was he."

"You're lucky."

Tory wondered if she'd imagined Devon's soft words, but she never had the chance to ask him. Briskly, he got to his feet and helped her to hers.

"Shall we unpack?" he asked politely.

Tory looked up into clear, unclouded green eyes and fought a sudden desire to hit him with the nearest handy object. Damn the man and his compelling, changeable, intriguing eyes! Like the smooth mirror surface of a lake they reflected calm and peace, then were abruptly disturbed by some pebble tossed in at random, causing ripples and changes . . . and puzzles.

Hastily, she pulled her hands from his. "Um . . . right."

If Devon hadn't realized early that morning that Tory Michaels was a complex woman, he very soon revised his initial impression of her. The first surprise had been the change in her physically: The survivor of the morning's war against wakefulness had become a beautiful woman whose entrancingly changeable eyes were vulnerable at first glance yet became guarded and controlled on closer inspection. There was a tense fragility about her that was reflected more in her still-ness than in anything she said, and he had to fight, more than once, an instinct to take her in his arms and soothe the troubled, puzzled frown from her brow.

He was too wise a man to ask her point-blank what disturbed her; the very few probing questions he'd ventured had met with definite resistance. And so he bided his time, concentrating first on maneuvering his way into her life in the most unthreatening way he could think of, without bothering to question his own motives too closely. That she distrusted him he knew; her reasons seemed more the result of past experience than anything he'd done or said. He filed that realization away in his brain and went about the business of finding out what he could about her by observing her and what she surrounded herself with.

She was upstairs when he began to unpack some of the crates in the barren downstairs room she had chosen for a work area. The carpet had been torn up to reveal a dully polished hardwood floor, and the only saving grace of the room to Devon's way of thinking was the row of floor-to-ceiling windows with a northern exposure lining an entire wall. He knew enough about art to understand why she'd chosen the space, and although she hadn't requested his help in unpacking the crates holding canvases, curiosity drove him to it.

He hesitated only momentarily, hoping devoutly that she wasn't the type of artist who'd resent his handling her work, then began to pry open crates carefully.

He propped the unframed canvases against one wall as he unpacked them, halting only when the first half-dozen were done. Then he stepped back to really look at them. They were a series, he realized immediately, meant to be viewed in a group. All were desert scenes, with cacti as the focus of the work. At first glance they were simply beautifully painted representations of the stark loneliness and majesty of deserts, but then Devon looked again, more carefully, and he recognized the quality that set this work and Tory's talent apart from anything he'd ever seen.

As he studied intently, the first painting of a cactus became instead the primitive form of a weeping woman. Head bowed with crushing grief, shoulders slumped, she was as starkly beautiful as the desert surrounding her, and just as desolate.

Devon ached instantly for her.

The second painting of the series depicted a cactus-man. Harsh, aloof, selfish, arrogant, there was cruelty and beauty in his face and pride in his stance. He seemed to gaze toward the horizon with the look of a conqueror, heavy-lidded eyes cold and calculating, and a clenched fist held delicate flowers crushed by unthinking, uncaring strength.

Devon hated him.

The third painting depicted two cacti rather than one; naturally, they must have grown from a common root. Artistically, Tory had interpreted lovers being torn from one another's arms. The woman was half turned, falling away from the man, her face a rough, thorny portrait of bewildered, stunned despair. The man reached for her, but one hand was a fist and the other a claw, both punishing although they didn't touch the woman. And his face was, like the second painting, a portrait of cruel beauty.

Devon hated the man with a hatred that surprised him.

Refusing to look at the remaining three paintings in that moment, he strode to the wall of windows and stared out. Raking a hand through his hair, he was startled at the tremor in his fingers, bewildered to realize that the paintings of powerful, cruel emotions had moved him so deeply.

He remained at the windows for several minutes, then finally took a deep breath and turned to the fourth painting.

The woman again. No longer grieving, she stood in the bleak desert and stared into a fiery red sunset. Her shoulders were set squarely with determination, her head high. And her face—her beautiful, hurt face—was still and empty and set in ragged pride.

Devon swallowed hard and looked at the fifth painting. The man. But this man could only be pitied rather than hated. His beauty was a soulless thing, his pride and strength only crutches. His cruelty was unthinking but obvious. He gazed off at a distant mountain, seeing not the beauty but the obstacle, not the majesty but the inconvenience. He saw with his eyes but not his heart.

The sixth painting depicted two cacti standing some few feet apart. The lovers again. She stood with her back to him, her face oddly featureless this time; there was something unformed about her, a lack of personality. No, Devon realized suddenly, a lack of *emotion*. Her beautiful face revealed only indifference. The man stood watching her, his thorny face puzzled, his body stiff with anger and . . . fear? He seemed a man who had lost something he had never known enough to value and who was now confused by his sense of loss.

Devon knew instinctively that Tory's remarkable insight into these particular emotions came from experience. And the harrowing emotions she had captured in oil revealed a depth of feeling he hadn't expected to find in her. Under the heading of "artistic intuition," of course, artists were expected to feel things very deeply; Devon believed that Tory's paintings—these, at least—came straight from the heart. Her heart.

Talented though she quite obviously was, these six paintings represented a clear coming to terms with her own feelings; they cried out with the mute violence that Tory's own controlled stillness would reject.

He knew, with the certainty of perception and a sudden muted anger of his own, that these paintings had shed Tory's tears for her.

"I didn't ask you to open these crates."

Devon turned slowly to face Tory. He heard no anger in her voice, but instinct warned him that these next few moments would determine whether or not he had truly begun to carve a place for himself here. "No. D'you mind?"

She was standing just inside the doorway, leaning

back against the jamb, and the wariness that disturbed him was present in her gray eyes. She glanced at the paintings. "Odd. You have them in the right order."

"D'you mind?" he repeated steadily.

"I suppose not."

He looked back at the paintings for a moment, then at her. "These are . . . extraordinary, Tory."

She inclined her head slightly, an abrupt gesture indicating thanks but also indicating a discomfort with the subject and perhaps even a trace of embarrassment for the naked emotions expressed in the paintings.

Devon probed cautiously, choosing to ignore—for the moment, at least—her clear unwillingness to discuss the paintings. "They're incredible. I've never seen cacti used to represent people before."

"Anthropomorphism," she said flatly. "Attributing human characteristics to nonhuman things. But you know that."

Devon was almost certain she had brought up the concept to promote a very neat change of subject. But he refused to chase wild geese.

"You've captured such a wide range of emotion," he said, watching her face intently. "It's harrowing just to *look* at each painting."

"Wasted emotion," she said abruptly.

"No. Not wasted." He gestured slightly. "You've created a—a series representing growth. From despair to rebirth. It's a brilliant achievement, Tory."

"Thank you." She was still abrupt.

Devon saw that her wariness was increasing, her lovely face beginning to shut down into an impenetrable mask, and he instantly abandoned the subject in order to prevent that. "I'll leave the rest in here to you; I imagine you'll want the workroom to be arranged a certain way," he said cheerfully. "How about in the living room? The paintings in those crates?"

The brief, puzzled frown disturbed her face, then vanished. She pushed herself away from the jamb and started out to the foyer. "They're not my work; I want to hang them in the living room."

Devon followed. "Okay. I'll go get some tools from the truck. Back in a minute."

Tory heard the front door close behind him. She moved slowly into the living room, automatically fishing the kitten from the opened crate he seemed to be stuck in. She set him on the floor and absently scolded him for scattering packing straw everywhere, then knelt and continued with the unpacking that Devon's arrival, their lunch, and her trip upstairs to put away linens had interrupted.

Her hands performed the tasks without direction from her mind, because her mind was reliving what she had seen moments ago in the workroom. The humorous, affable Devon had not gazed at her paintings; he had looked at them, instead, with the intensity she had seen once before. And mixed with that had been the astute intelligence she mistrusted.

Sharp enough to cut himself...

But he had thrown her off guard again, changing the subject instantly and distracting her attention. Damn the man. Tory gazed blindly down at a jade figurine for a long time, looking up only when she heard him returning.

"Got 'em," he told her easily, setting a toolbox down on the floor near the French doors. "I'll unpack the crates first; then you can tell me where you want everything."

"What d'you do for a living?" she demanded, ignoring his words.

Devon looked down at her with a raised brow. "What brought that on?" he asked.

"Answer the question," she requested, thinking of the shrewdness and sharp intelligence that were curiously at odds with his affability.

He stepped over to a crate, beginning to pry it open. "I'll let you guess," he told her maddeningly.

"Devon—"

"Hey!" He reached down suddenly to pluck the kitten from the left leg of his pants, where tiny claws were engaged in trying to climb. "Hang on to Dumbo here, will you? Try to convince him I'm not a tree."

Distracted once again, Tory accepted the kitten and held him in her lap. "Don't call him that," she said, pulling gently at the overlarge ears of her new pet. "You'll hurt his feelings."

"He didn't do much for my leg," Devon pointed out politely.

"You can take care of yourself."

"So can he. Obviously."

Tory stared up into limpid green eyes for a moment, then announced firmly, "You changed the subject."

"Did I?" he wondered vaguely.

She sighed. "Look, if you don't want me to know what you do for a living, just *say* that, okay?"

"I don't want you to know what I do for a living."

"Why not?"

"Mystery."

"I think we've had this conversation before."

"It does sound familiar, doesn't it?"

Tory decided that two could play his game of innocent subject-changes. It wouldn't make her come out on top, since she *still* didn't know what he did for a living, but at least she stood a chance of keeping the dratted man as off balance as he kept her. "Whiskey," she said calmly.

"You feel the need for a drink?" Devon asked politely.

She held the kitten up to her neck, where he burrowed happily beneath her hair. "His name is Whiskey."

Irritatingly, Devon appeared as evenly balanced as always.

"S'fine by me. I won't ask how he happened to 'name himself' Whiskey, though."

Tory abandoned any further attempt to throw Devon off balance. There appeared to be a trick to the thing, requiring a mastery she didn't—yet—possess. "Careful with that," she directed as he began removing a large framed painting from the opened crate. "It's older than both of us." She set Whiskey to one side and shooed him gently away.

Holding the painting carefully, Devon stared at it for a long moment, then looked down at Tory. "She has to be an ancestor."

"Great-Great-Grandmother Magda."

He whistled softly. "You're the living spit of her."

"I know. And the odd thing is that nobody else in the family has ever looked even remotely like her. Daddy was a brown-eyed blond, and *his* father was a redhead."

"So you're a descendant through the male line?"

"Uh-huh. My great-great-grandfather—Magda's husband—was dark, too, but he was Irish-dark. Where Magda was born nobody knows; she was a Gypsy." Tory smiled suddenly. "And that ends the family history lesson for today."

Devon continued to study the painting. The resemblance, he thought, was truly remarkable. From the fine blue-black raven's-wing hair to the heart-shaped face and the eyes that seemed to subtly change color even as he stared, Tory was the living image of her great-great-grandmother. The painting had been done when Magda was roughly Tory's age, youth blending smoothly into womanhood. The clothing of an earlier era, curiously enough, enhanced the likeness. Magda's expression alone differed from Tory's. There was no wariness in the Gypsy's face, only the serenity of certain self-knowledge; there was no guarded firmness in her curved lips.

If Magda had ever been hurt by life, she had put it behind her and forgotten it.

Noticing his continued interest in the painting, Tory, puzzled, resumed the history lesson. "I never knew her; she died before I was born. Daddy said she was the stillest woman he'd ever known. Never nervous, never restless. And she adored her husband."

Devon took a deep breath and released it slowly.

"You're lucky to have this. Not many of us can point to . . . tangible roots."

"Can you?" she asked, suddenly curious.

He shook his head slightly. "No. I never even knew my grandparents."

Tory, thinking of the rich lore handed down to her by generations, the stories and legends and personalities, felt sorry for Devon. What a lot he had missed out on!

"Where d'you want this hung?" he asked.

She pointed to the wall between two front windows. "There." She watched him carefully hang the painting, making sure its anchor to the wall was secure, and felt her interest in the man growing. This time she didn't try to deny that interest; she merely considered it.

Why did the man fascinate her? Because he was complex, a puzzle—she knew that. Because the affable and courteous gentleman he was on the surface masked, she knew, something else, something more intriguing. The urge to paint him had not diminished; she *did* ignore that. What disturbed her now was that her interest in him was the purely human and feminine attraction to the handsome and charming man standing just across the room.

Other than taking her hands briefly, he hadn't so much as touched her. And yet . . . Tory was almost painfully aware of his every move and gesture. She pondered that, trying to be analytical about it. Trying— and failing. She was too aware of the man to back off and view him objectively. She knew only that something about him, perhaps a hint of vulnerability she sensed more than saw, got to her.

And then, quite suddenly, Tory realized in disgust that she was being entirely too paranoid about Devon York. Whether or not she was attracted to him, Devon was simply a very nice, unusual man with time on his hands who'd decided to help out a lady in distress; after her description of her chaotic morning, he probably thought she needed a keeper. Perhaps he even felt—ridiculous, but possible—responsible for her just because she happened to have bought a house formerly owned by his new sister-in-law.

Whatever his reasoning, Devon obviously had nothing more on his mind than companionship and a means to wile away his—his what?—vacation? Anything else was just a product of her overactive imagination. Tory chided herself mentally and tried to relax. But that was difficult, because although Devon's attitude seemed perfectly straightforward, her own was becoming increasingly confused.

"Tory?"

'Hmm?" She blinked up at him. He had hung the portrait and now stood a couple of feet away, looking down at her. "Oh, sorry. You were saying?"

Devon looked hurt. "The least you can do is pay attention to my proposals!" he complained woefully.

She blinked again. "Sorry. I'm all ears."

In an aggrieved voice, he repeated his proposal. "I *said* that you really should marry me, because then I could share your ancestors. I mean, since I don't have any of my own."

"Of course you have ancestors," she said reasonably. "You wouldn't be here if you didn't. You just don't know who they were, that's all."

"Whatever. And you didn't respond to the proposal."

"Then I will. If you want ancestors, take up genealogy."

Devon shook his head. "You're cruel."

"I know. It's terrible, isn't it?"

He sighed heavily. "I'll say. Ah, well, what's next?"

Having finally decided to relax and enjoy Devon's relatively unthreatening company, Tory found the remainder of the day a lot of fun. They put the house in order in an astonishingly short time and without the exhaustion she would have suffered had she done the work alone. There was still a lot to be done, as Devon pointed out helpfully, but progress through each room was no longer impeded by crates and boxes.

Paintings and prints were ranged along the walls, propped up beneath the places where they'd later be hung; figurines, vases, and other ornaments were grouped together on tables and shelves, ready to be placed in as yet unacquired curio cabinets; Tory's sparse furniture was placed where she decided—for now, anyway—she wanted it.

Tory and Devon worked both together and separately during the day; more often than not, they busied themselves in different rooms. Devon had quickly discovered her rather extensive stereo system and had loaded the turntable with a stack of semiclassical albums. So music filled the house.

And laughter. Devon came in search of her at least once every hour, voicing a new and creative proposal and then retreating with a hangdog expression after hearing her polite rejection. He called out cheerful questions about her possessions from time to time, seemingly fascinated by the heirlooms being steadily unpacked. He found a stack of yellowed tarot cards and requested that she tell his fortune—being the great-great-granddaughter of a Gypsy, after all. Matching his solemnity, Tory promised to do so one day.

It was fairly late when they quit for the day and shared a hastily and jointly prepared supper of steak and salad. Conversation was cheerful, a bit weary, and very general—not a disturbing word or puzzling look exchanged between them. They shared the cleaning chores, still companionable.

And then Devon left with a promise to return in the morning and an easy good-bye.

Tory automatically made sure the house was locked up, double-checked to see that Whiskey had a bowl of kitten food in the kitchen in case hunger pangs attacked during the night, and then trailed up to her bedroom.

The bed was assembled, thanks to Devon, and neatly made, her clothing put away in drawers and closet. She took a hot shower, donned a filmy nylon gown, and went back into her bedroom to find that Whiskey had climbed onto the bed with what must have been a heroic effort and was waiting for her.

"If you get lost during the night and can't find your box," she told him sleepily as she drew back the covers, "don't wake me up."

Ignoring the order, the kitten squirmed beneath the covers and curled up at her side. His rumbling purr was muffled by blankets but still audible, and Tory giggled drowsily. She lay back on the pillows, then sat up again abruptly as she felt something hard beneath them. Cautiously sliding a hand underneath, she found a book.

It was a small, exquisitely bound volume of poetry. Love poetry.

Tory knew each and every book she owned, and she was positive this wasn't one of them. She opened it, puzzled, and discovered a bookmark placed precisely at the poem titled "How Do I Love Thee." The bookmark bore the glittering representation of a unicorn and the words "May all your dreams come true."

No matter how efficient or always-prepared Devon was, Tory was reasonably sure he wouldn't carry such a thing around in his pocket—which meant that he'd been a very busy man between his first and second trips to her house. She revisited one of her favorite poems and then read a few others, trying to convince herself that this was merely a continuation of Devon's exercises in creative proposing. Nothing more. Nothing more than that.

She almost convinced herself.

The next few days very nearly repeated the pattern of that first one. Devon always arrived reasonably late in the morning, giving Tory time to be up and awake, and he always brought food—prepared or ready to be—with him. He was preceded each morning by a delivery man bearing silk flowers of various types and arrangements, and nothing Tory could say in protest had any effect on the arrival of the gifts. And somehow, without her seeing him, Devon always managed to leave something beneath her pillow. A heart-shaped box of candy. A silk scarf. An I.D. bracelet with her name on one side and "My Bright Particular Star" on the other.

Tory had easily completed the quotation in her mind: "That I should love a bright, particular star and think to wed it." And she convinced herself yet again that he was still practicing his proposals. Just practicing.

Because Devon was rapidly becoming the best friend she'd had in years. He made her laugh. He kept her on her toes mentally, since she never knew when he'd suddenly turn shrewd eyes on her or when his deep voice would become suddenly intense. Those little "lapses" never lasted long, and they intrigued her because she had quickly realized that Devon was usually in complete control of himself.

But in spite of her uneasiness regarding those lapses, Tory thoroughly enjoyed his company. She was in no hurry to go back to work; he certainly seemed in no hurry. So they leisurely put her house in order and spent long hours talking about casual, unimportant things.

And if Tory realized, at some deep and vital level, that she was falling in love with him, she banished that half-formed realization from her heart and mind.

Because Devon never bestowed anything more than the most casual of touches, and it was quite obvious that he was merely a man with time on his hands. Nothing more.

And she banished any thoughts of love because, aside from his own obvious disinterest, she had no emotional energy to waste on a relationship; she needed all she had for her work. *That* emotional energy could be channeled into a useful outlet, and she knew all too well that any other outlet was a baited trap for the unwary.

Not for Tory Michaels.

She had gone through an emotional catharsis two years ago, and once was enough for her. The violence of her own feelings had shocked and frightened her, and she never wanted to experience another such loss of control. Ever.

Chapter 4

"YOU PROMISED TO tell my fortune," he said firmly, handing her the yellowed tarot cards.

They were in her den, sitting on the comfortable couch before a newly built roaring fire. Whiskey was curled up on a pillow by the hearth, close enough to the fire to feel the heat but not close enough to burn his tail, and two half-empty wineglasses reposed on the coffee table. It was past nine o'clock at night, and thunder had been rumbling warningly for some time. Tory listened as the wind picked up outside, then looked at Devon. "You sure picked a good night for it."

"What we *really* need," he said in a theatrically throbbing voice, "is for the lights to go out."

At that exact moment, they did.

There was a deafening crash of thunder, and brilliant lightning lit their still faces. Then the wind howled eerily, and rain began to pelt the house as if in attack.

Mildly, Tory said, "Your timing is perfect."

"I'll be damned," he said blankly.

The firelight cast a flickering golden glow over the room, leaving corners in shadow, but even the darkest recesses were washed white when lightning bent its frowning glare on them.

"Sure you want me to read your fortune?" she asked wryly.

"I'm sure." Devon winced slightly as thunder crashed again, then looked at her. She was lovelier than ever in the fire's soft glow, and he found himself fighting urges even more powerful than those he'd fought for days. Resolutely, he kept his mind on the subject at hand. "But first, tell me if I should take this seriously or if it's just a parlor game. I mean, did you inherit more than black hair and strange Gypsy eyes from Magda?"

Tory turned the cards in her hands for a moment, staring down at them. The firelight had turned her eyes to silver and carved hollows beneath her cheek-bones, lending her normally piquant face an air of mystery that was perfectly suited to the stormy night and his stormy emotions.

"I guess it depends on what you believe," she said finally, wondering if she should tell him that, Gypsy ancestor notwithstanding, she'd never tried to tell anyone's fortune before. Oh, she'd learned the most elementary rules for setting out the first several cards; Ouija boards and tarot cards had been something of a fad when she was a teenager. But aside from keeping a tarot deck, she'd never indulged in things mystical. She decided not to mention that little fact. Devon York wasn't the only one who could hanker for a bit of mystery, after all.

"What do *you* believe?" he asked softly.

She looked at him with limpid eyes and said in what she hoped was a mysterious voice, "I'm descended from a Gypsy, remember? I believe in a lot of things I can't see with my eyes or hold in my hands." She held out the cards to him, hoping her memory would serve her well. "Now, tap the deck and then cut it."

Wordlessly, he followed her directions.

Tory dealt the cards in a pattern on the coffee table, explaining what each card meant—of itself and in relation to those surrounding it—as she turned it face up. It wasn't difficult to ad lib, since each card's illustration rather graphically reminded her of its most obvious meaning.

"Your past. Something divided. Strife. Opposition. Then—decision. Following a—new path. No, making a path of your own. Yourself still divided, still not whole. Your present. Suspension. A time of waiting. Still not whole. Your future, shown by three cards. The first, a storm, danger. The second, a journey. The third, the sun, coming gratification. An end of waiting. Wholeness."

When Tory turned up the next card, she fell silent, staring down at it. It figured, she thought wryly; she *would* have to turn up that particular card!

"Don't stop now," Devon murmured. He, too, was staring down at the card. He didn't know much about tarot cards, but he knew a representation of entwined lovers when he saw one.

Tory said nothing about that card, but she turned up the next one, flanking the card bearing the lovers. "This is your card," she said carefully. "It represents you." Then she turned up another card, placing it, also, next to the lovers. Hastily, she swept the cards up, saying a bit breathlessly, "And that's all."

But Devon had seen that last card; it bore the image of a dark-haired woman with mysterious eyes, and he didn't have to be a wizard or the descendant of a Gypsy to guess what it meant.

"So we're going to be lovers," he said calmly.

"You and a dark-haired woman, perhaps," she said instantly, shuffling the cards with restless, jerky movements. "Not me."

He reached out to cover her hands with one of his. "Shouldn't we be sure about that? Read your fortune now."

Tory stared down at his hand for a long moment, then took a deep breath. "All right." She tried to tell herself the cards were virtually meaningless, superstition at best, but her inner arguments lacked conviction. She'd spent many a childhood hour watching her father sculpt and listening to his stories about the Gypsies—stories he had believed. And when one hears stories from a parent one adores, belief is automatic and enduring; part of her had always believed.

Forcing her fingers to be steady, she tapped the

deck, cut it, and began to deal, speaking evenly.

"My past. Happiness. Then disillusionment. Solitude." She hesitated at the next card, then continued firmly, "Not whole. My present. Suspension. A—a time of waiting."

Dizzily, she wondered at the similarity of their fortunes. She knew it couldn't be wishful thinking on her part, since the cards could only be interpreted the way they fell. And her interpretation of them, she knew, was correct. She went on determinedly.

"My future. A storm. A journey. The sun, coming gratification. An end of waiting. Wholeness." She turned up the next card.

The lovers.

"The next card is me." She turned it up slowly, not surprised to see the dark-haired woman. She placed it beside the lovers, then turned up the next card and placed it on the other side of the lovers.

It was Devon's card.

"You see?" he murmured softly. "We are meant to be lovers."

Tory was determined to treat the matter lightly. "The odds against that must be astronomical," she said easily, sweeping the cards up. "I mean, two fortunes told, one right after the other, and both so similar. And the bits about storms. It's uncanny, isn't it?"

"Not if you believe in fate and Gypsy fortune-telling."

She slid the cards back into their box and placed it on the coffee table. "We live in the twentieth century, Devon," she said a bit more breathlessly than she'd intended. "Fortune-telling belongs in carnival side-shows. You don't really believe—"

"Don't I?"

Quite suddenly, she found herself hauled against the solid wall of his chest, and through the thin material of his shirt she could feel an erratic pounding that must have been his heart. Her fingers moved instinctively, probing the muscled firmness covering that heart. And then she realized what she was doing. "Devon—"

"I believe," he murmured huskily, his lips feathering lightly along her jawline, "in fortune-telling, my little tzigane, my little *zingara*. I believe. Especially when it only confirms what I've felt myself since the morning I saw a plaid robe and a purple towel and strange Gypsy eyes."

"You—you never showed it," she managed weakly, aware that her head was tilting back to allow him more room to explore and unable to do a damn thing about her body's reaction. "Deceiver . . . you're an unscrupulous, conniving, deceitful—"

"Hungry man," he finished with a low laugh. "Hungry for a *zingara*'s touch."

"What . . . does that mean? *Zingara?*" She was stingingly aware of his lips moving toward the corner of her own like a whisper of promise. And she knew she should be thinking very seriously about what was happening, but somehow that seemed impossible. Later. She'd think about it later. *When it's too late to think!* her mind sneered—but she didn't listen.

"It's Italian for Gypsy," Devon murmured, his lips

hovering just above hers. He guided her gently back until she was lying on the couch with him stretched out close beside her, their bodies pressed together. "I've never kissed a *zingara,*" he breathed.

Tory stared, wide-eyed, even after his lips touched hers. His face was so fascinating, half in shadow and half glowing golden from the firelight . . . And then her eyes drifted closed as a warmth having nothing to do with the fire began spreading through her.

He was gentle, almost hesitant, as if he felt that to move too quickly would be to frighten her. His lips moved tentatively over hers, probing, shaping, listening with other senses. His tongue traced the sensitive inner surface of her lips in a searching little caress that brought the blood pounding to her head.

Resistance had never been on Tory's mind, and although the sneering little voice within her idly condemned her for it, she could hardly help but respond. This fascinating, changeable man had somehow turned the tables on her yet again, knocking her off balance with his sudden desire. Her fingers slid up his chest, curling to dig into his shoulders as emptiness yawned abruptly inside of her.

Her mouth bloomed beneath his, warming, becoming hungry. The woodsy scent of his cologne filled her senses, transporting her in time and place to enchanted forests where elves laughed and Gypsies danced. The warmth of those pagan campfires ran hotly through her veins, igniting feelings she'd not known existed within her. And she knew now why Magda smiled with such serene mystery in the portrait, knew now what the Gypsy woman had also known.

She had never felt this way before.

Not even with...

Tory gasped as his lips left hers to burn a trail down the V neckline of her sweater, striving desperately to push the half-formed realization out of her mind. Nonsense. She barely knew this man.

But his lips were a brand against her flesh, a brand of possession, and she could feel the tremor in his body answer her own. Thunder rumbled outside as his fingers slid beneath the sweater to touch the soft, quivering skin of her stomach, and his hand was a live wire to shock and ignite.

Too fast, it was happening too fast, and somehow they had to slow down...

"Zingara..."

The distraction came rather suddenly and from an unexpected source, and Tory felt an overwhelming urge to giggle. "Um... Devon?"

"Hmm?"

"Why are you wearing an earring?"

His head lifted abruptly, the hand beneath her sweater transferring its attention to his ear, where her fingers still toyed gently.

"Ah, hell," he muttered, clearly torn between disgust and chagrin. "I forgot all about that!"

It wasn't much as earrings went—just a golden loop so fine as to be virtually invisible. Tory hadn't even noticed it until her searching fingers had encountered it. "I *have* to know why you're wearing an earring," she said solemnly.

Devon sighed, then smiled ruefully down at her.

"Not because I wanted to, believe me. I was . . . uh . . . made a sort of honorary member of a tribe, and the earring is the . . . badge of membership. It would have been an insult to refuse, and afterward I just forgot the damn thing."

"Tribe?" She stared up at him, bemused. "Of Indians?"

"You could say that. Strictly speaking. It was in South America a few months back."

After a moment, and very calmly, Tory said, "If you don't tell me right now—this very minute—what you do for a living, I shall quite probably kill you."

"It's very dull," he evaded.

"Devon."

"*Very* dull. No mystery."

"Devon!"

"Hell. I'm an archaeologist."

Tory gazed up at his face, seeing there an odd sort of defensiveness, and she added another piece to the puzzle this man was. After a moment, she said dryly, "I'd hardly call deserts, sheikhs, ambassadors, and honorary memberships in native tribes *dull*."

He looked at her, one green eye brilliant in the firelight and the other in shadow, and the tension she had seen in his face seemed to drain away. "You wouldn't?" He hesitated, then added doggedly, "It usually is, you know. Dull. Hours of repetitive work, usually with little gain. Living in tents. Wearing a ton of dust or sand in your clothes. Eating out of cans because God ony knows what's in the local community stewpot."

"Studying the past," she said softly. "Piecing together a culture dead for centuries. Touching a life that was. Dull? Oh, no, Devon—not dull."

She touched the tiny golden earring that so nearly matched his golden flesh, and her vivid imagination conjured an image of another pagan campfire, this one surrounded by faces solemn with ceremony. She smiled suddenly. "Did it hurt?"

His fingers moved to lightly fondle one of her own pierced lobes. "You tell me," he said wryly.

"It did!" She laughed.

"Damned right!" Then he sobered, gazing down at her with a curious wonder in his face. "Why didn't I meet you ten years ago?" he mused softly.

"What was her name?" Tory asked quietly.

He was obviously startled. "Her?"

"The woman who convinced you your work was dull."

"Oh. Her. Lisa." He touched her face gently. "And you're a very perceptive lady, *zingara.*"

"I just hope she—didn't hurt you too much," Tory said a bit uncertainly, wondering at her own words.

"I survived."

Before Tory could question him, Devon had turned the tables on her yet again. "And what about you, *zingara?* What was *his* name?"

"Who?"

"The cactus-man. The man with the beautiful, cruel face who hurt you."

Laughing a little shakily, she said, "We seem to be a perceptive pair tonight."

"Tory . . ."

She took a deep breath, keeping her arms around

his neck because there was an odd security in that and because the pagan fires that had warmed her blood still flickered beneath his verbal probing. "His name was Jordan. And he hurt me only because I was too blind to see him for what he really was."

"And do you still hurt because of him?" Devon asked quietly.

Tory hesitated, then answered honestly. "No. but he left me . . . wary."

"Wary enough to fight the cards' prediction?" He watched her face intently, looking for a return of the mask. But it didn't return. Instead, she looked up at him with a new vulnerability in her Gypsy eyes, and he felt his heart lurch inside him.

"I don't know, Devon."

And she didn't know. Not that. All she knew was that she would be taking a huge gamble if she let Devon into her mind and heart. Because once that happened, she'd never be rid of him. Unlike Jordan, Devon would become a part of her, and she knew it. She'd carry him with her all the days of her life. Already he was under her skin . . .

"Then we'll take our time, *zingara*." He kissed her very gently with no demand, his fingers smoothing the fine black hair away from her face. "We'll take all the time you need."

Tory stared up at him, feeling the pagan pounding in her veins, and marveled at his patience. Or perhaps he just didn't feel the same desire that she did? "'You're a better man than I am, Gunga Din,'" she said tremulously.

Devon looked at her, his green eyes probing with

the shrewdness that no longer surprised her. Then, softly, he said, "There's another quotation from Kipling. 'Through the Jungle very softly flits a shadow and a sigh—He is Fear, O Little Hunter, he is Fear!' I've seen that shadow on your face, *zingara*. I don't like it there. I don't want it there. So I'll wait. Even if I have to lash myself to a mast in the meantime."

Just as softly, her eyes gazing into the jewel-green brilliance of his, she said, "Ulysses had himself lashed to a mast so he could hear the siren song but not go overboard to his death."

Devon nodded. "Don't you know?" he murmured. "You're a living siren song, little *zingara*. But it isn't death I fear; it's seeing you turn away from me. So. I wait."

Tory was bewildered by his quiet intensity, by the stark truth in his eyes. It was almost as if—But no. He hadn't mentioned love. Only desire. Her body curved into his as he stretched out fully beside her; they both faced the fire in the hearth, and she could feel his heart beating strongly against her back, feel his breath stirring her hair, feel his powerful arms wrapped around her. But she could no longer look into his face, and for that she was grateful.

She listened to the inner voice now, listened to the warnings her mind had been screaming, heard but ignored, for some time now.

Devon York was a dangerous man.

An insidiously dangerous man.

And she was a fool.

What did he want of her? Obviously he wanted to

know her in a way only one other man had known her. He wanted her, and he was prepared to wait for what he wanted. Why? Because she didn't think his profession dull and boring? Ridiculous. That was ridiculous. Because the cards foretold that they would be lovers? Even more ridiculous. Devon was certainly a rational man, an intellectual man; he wouldn't put faith in such nonsense as tarot cards. Even if they *were* read by the descendant of a Gypsy.

Tory stared fixedly at the fire's golden flame until everything but that became hazy and unreal.

He wanted her.

He would wait.

He loves me . . .

He loves me not . . .

The flames wavered before her eyes, filling her vision and her mind. It didn't matter, really. Not really. Because, of course, she didn't love him. She wouldn't let herself love him. He was a complex, deceptively unthreatening man who bore scars. The distaste and probable ridicule of the woman who had thought his profession dull had left scars. How deep those scars went, she had no idea. But they existed. Chinks in his armor.

He was a strong man, was Devon York. Intelligent, witty, honest, determined, perhaps even ruthless in his own deceptively quiet way. And that strength attracted her, intrigued her. But it was his vulnerability, the chinks in his armor that she feared. Strength could be met with strength, but vulnerability . . . vulnerability could not be defended against. It was the most devastating weapon of all, the one that would defeat her in the end if anything did.

Not, of course, that she loved him.

That was absurd.

Remember the saying, her sneering inner voice warned: *Fool me once, shame on you. Fool me twice, shame on me*.

Was she going to allow herself to make another emotional judgment that would devastate her? Would she let her hard-won rationality be overborne by the fleeting pleasures of reckless love?

No, Tory Michaels didn't intend to be fooled twice. And God knew that Jordan had come into her life just as unthreateningly as Devon. With his charming smiles and his witty remarks, he had effortlessly captured her interest and her love. And when that love withered and died a painful death in the face of stark truth and understanding, it was Jordan who emerged unscathed. Not she.

Blinking, Tory brought the fire back into focus. Well, she decided firmly, this time she would emerge unscathed. Except that there wouldn't be anything to emerge *from*, because ... No. No, there *would* be something to emerge from; she was already involved with Devon.

All right! she thought fiercely. All *right*, then! She couldn't deceive herself into believing she wasn't attracted to the man; why not name that attraction *desire* and be done with it?

But it would be all right. Just a brief interlude before Devon returned to his deserts and ruins and she to her art. Just a brief interlude, and God knew she was entitled, wasn't she? She should take him at face value, accept the warmth and companionship and desire he offered, and remain heart-whole when it was over.

And she could do that.

If she didn't fall in love with him.

Tory felt his heart beating against her, felt the even rise and fall of his chest that meant he was probably asleep, and she wondered again at his control. Devon York seemed a man superbly equipped to walk confidently through life, scars notwithstanding. A man in complete control of himself and his life. A man almost perpetually on balance.

She listened to the thunder rumbling outside, to the rain and wind and to her misgivings and fears. She looked down at the arms holding her securely, aware that the pagan fire within her, though banked by rational thoughts, still smoldered.

And when sleep claimed her sometime later, it brought no counsel.

Always reluctant to face a new day, Tory fought waking as long as possible. When she did finally manage to unglue her eyelids, she noticed several things. The first was that Whiskey had apparently decided sometime during the night to bed down on her chest, since he was curled up mere inches from her chin, sound asleep. The second was that she was on the couch, lying mostly on her back. The third was that it was a sunny, stormless morning.

The fourth was that Devon still lay beside her; he was poised on an elbow and was smiling down at her with what she irritably felt to be an ungodly amount of morning cheer.

"Good morning," he murmured.

"Hello," she responded blearily.

"It's a beautiful day," he offered.

"Interested in a rebuttal to that?"

Devon laughed.

Tory winced; it just wasn't decent, she thought, to be so bright-eyed so early in the day. "Is today really *necessary?*" she wondered plaintively. "Couldn't we skip it and go straight to tomorrow?"

"That's not the way it works," he explained solemnly.

"It's the way it should work. In fact, today should always be outlawed in favor of tomorrow."

"You sound like a poster I saw once."

"Oh?"

"Uh-huh. It ran something like: 'I'd like the day better if it began later.'"

"I'll drink to that."

"The sun isn't over the yardarm yet."

"It must be over the yardarm *somewhere.*"

"This is true."

Quite abruptly, Tory remembered the night before, and it must have shown on her face or in her eyes because Devon immediately leaned down and kissed her gently, the scrape of his morning beard an oddly sensuous little caress.

"Don't panic on me now," he murmured.

"I never panic," she managed staunchly.

"I know." He was smiling. "You never panic and you never cry. You're a tough lady, aren't you, *zingara?*"

"Very tough." Tory didn't know whom she was trying to convince: Devon or herself.

"Then tell me, tough lady, what're you afraid of?"

Tory stared up at him, aware that she was in no shape to answer that very pointed question in anything but a very revealing manner. But he was looking down at her gravely now, and she suddenly decided that it might, perhaps, be best to lay her cards on the table for him to see.

"You," she said starkly.

A frown drew his brows together. "Why?"

She searched through the list of reasons, condensing all of them, finally, under one neat heading. "Because I don't understand you."

"Is that so important?" he asked with a quizzical half-smile. "I don't completely understand you either, *zingara*. But we have time."

"Do we?"

"Sure."

Tory remembered her advice to herself of the night before and decided somewhat grimly to follow it. She'd take him at face value and accept what he offered. And if a part of her was still intent on understanding him, then so be it. She wanted to understand her friend.

Before he became her lover.

Chapter 5

TORY STOOD IN the kitchen, drinking coffee and staring down at Whiskey as he hungrily lapped his breakfast. Devon had solemnly asked to borrow her razor and then gone upstairs to shave, while she had contented herself with brushing her hair and starting the coffee.

She was, of course, only just beginning to wake up now. And when he came into the kitchen a few minutes later, she instantly said, "Never, *never* ask serious questions before I've had my coffee. It's unfair and ungentlemanly."

"Want another shot at the question?" he asked politely.

Tory sighed. "No. Just don't do that to me again."

"My word of honor. Now, how about breakfast?"

"How about it?"

He chuckled softly, gazing at her with bright eyes. "It's up to me, huh?"

"You *know* I hate cooking," she said patiently, "at the best of times. And breakfast is hardly the best of times. Don't expect the impossible, pal."

Devon sighed in manful long-suffering. "I guess I'd better get to work, then."

"You do that."

Laughing, Devon opened the refrigerator and began removing items for breakfast. "By the way, since you're obviously waking up now—"

"I'm working on it."

"—I just thought I'd offer to marry you. I mean, since I compromised you by spending the night here and everything."

Tory fiercely steadied her heart by reminding herself that Devon was simply still "practicing" his proposals. "In another life," she said calmly.

Breaking eggs into a bowl, Devon laughed again. "It's a good thing I don't have ego problems," he said philosophically.

She poured another cup of coffee for herself, then one for him, adding dryly, "Besides, I could never marry anyone who's so damned cheerful in the morning. It's indecent."

"If I learned to sleep late, would you marry me?" he asked anxiously.

Tory fell back on a proverb: "You can't teach an old dog new tricks."

"I'm not an old dog!"

"The point stands."

Devon caught her hand after she set his coffee on

the counter, drawing her close to his side and bending his head to kiss her with deliberate thoroughness. "I'd be happy to learn from you," he murmured.

"Um . . . the bacon's burning," she said, wondering with a definitely put-upon feeling how her arms had worked themselves up around his neck.

His smile glinted at her before one hand slid down to pat her briefly on the fanny. "All right, *zingara*, have it your own way."

As soon as he released her, Tory retreated to the counter across the room, picking up her coffee cup and frowning at him. "Ungentlemanly!" she accused a bit breathlessly.

Devon was unrepentant. "All's fair, tough lady. All's fair."

If Tory had vaguely supposed that there would be little change in Devon's behavior after his briefly unleashed passion of the night before, she very quickly discovered just how wrong supposition could be.

For one thing, the intensity she had seen only occasionally until now became an ever-present thing in his green eyes; he looked at her more often, and the warmth of that intensity was unsettling. And for another thing, his touch-me-not attitude of the first days vanished as if it had been a figment of her imagination; he couldn't seem to stop touching her, however casual that touch might be.

He kept her unsettled that day. He made her laugh, often in spite of herself. He treated her as if she were a cherished treasure one moment and a sparring partner the next. He was alternately a pal and a lover, joking one moment and kissing her until she was dizzy the next.

And Tory found herself swept along helplessly in his confusing wake.

"You're being ungentlemanly again!" she accused after one rather potent attack on her equilibrium.

Devon managed to look both wounded and triumphant at the same time. "I never claimed to be a gentleman."

"And I never claimed to be an idiot! Devon—"

"D'you realize your eyes sparkle when you're annoyed with me?"

"I'll bet they *threw* you out of that desert!"

"Sticks and stones."

She narrowed her eyes at him. "Careful. The life you save may well be your own."

"Marry me and I'll take you away from all this."

"Are you kidding? With you around, there's no place to go but crazy!"

"Now you've cut me to the quick."

"I don't think you *have* a quick. Except—Devon!"

"What?"

"Quick hands! For heaven's sake . . ."

"Kiss me, Kate."

"I'm not Kate, and you're not taming a shrew, dammit."

"I'm beginning to think that I am . . ."

Tory enjoyed the good-natured fencing, the innuendos; she wasn't about to deny, even to herself, that she enjoyed his kisses and his touch. But she was still puzzled and a bit unsettled by at least one facet of his personality: his control. It was always there, always present beneath the banter and the intensity. She didn't know why it bothered her so much, except perhaps because she felt he was holding back something of himself.

And that brought echoes of her relationship with Jordan and the qualities in him she'd not seen until it was too late. She knew it was hardly fair of her to expect Devon to bare his soul while she kept her own tightly wrapped and hidden, but her instincts for self-preservation urged that very one-sided arrangement over fairness.

So she held on to her willpower, resisting both him and herself, playing with fire but never coming close enough to be burned. And that night, as in the nights that followed, a part of her wished Devon would lose his control—not only because she distrusted it but also because his loss of control might well free her from the decision he awaited so patiently.

A decision she was still unwilling to make.

But she came to realize, reluctantly, that he had meant what he said about waiting. And that his control, like a solid protective wall with spikes on top, was going to withstand the test of time.

After four days, she came very close to breaking.

He was kissing her good night at her door, as he had every night, and Tory wasn't looking forward to sleeping in her lonely bed. "Why don't you throw me over your saddle and gallop off into the night?" she demanded plaintively.

His hands linked together loosely at the small of

her back, Devon smiled down at her. "Why don't you throw yourself over my saddle, and we'll gallop off into the night," he suggested softly.

Tory glared at him. "Whatever happened to the hunter's instincts?" she muttered irritably. "Yours ought to be quivering by now."

"They are," he confirmed affably. "But I'm the hunter who waits, remember?"

"Why?"

"Why do I wait?" Devon laughed softly and branded a last hard, possessive kiss on her lips. "You'll have to make like Kipling's mongoose, *zingara:* Go and find out. 'Night." And then he was gone.

Tory fought a childish impulse to kick the door. Sighing, she wandered into the living room, picking Whiskey from where he lay in her favorite chair and sitting down with him in her lap. She watched her hands shake for a few wry moments, then stared up at Magda's portrait.

The Gypsy woman, smiling with her serene, mysteriously knowing gaze, stared back.

"I'm acting like a child, Magda," Tory murmured. "I *know* I'm acting like a child. I'm an adult, for godsake. An observant, analytical artist. So why do I feel threatened every time he reminds me it's my decision? Why do I want *him* to be responsible for whatever happens between us?"

Magda continued to smile serenely.

Tory went on trying to sort out her own thoughts and motivations.

"Am I afraid of making the choice because of what happened with Jordan? Do I want someone else to blame this time if it all goes wrong? Or ... do I some-how trust Devon more than I trust myself? He has ancient eyes, Magda, ancient knowing eyes, as the Gypsy men must have had. I think he sees me in a way no one else ever has. And when I look at him, I see ..."

What did she see? A strong man. A vulnerable man. A laughing man. An intense man. Sensitivity. A subtle ruthlessness. Tenderness. Passion. A man who walked like a cat or a king. A master gamesman who knew when to hold his cards close to his chest. A man who stole her breath and left her dizzy. A man who continued to send flowers each day so that now her new house was bright and cheerful with their silky color and permanence.

Sighing, Tory pushed the reflections from her mind. She felt restless; she knew she'd be unable to sleep. After a moment, she rose and carried Whiskey in search of something to occupy her mind, returning to her chair with a thick volume of poetry. Then she determinedly bent her mind to memorizing certain pertinent verses—just in case Devon continued to practice his proposals.

And when she finally did wander up the stairs to her bed and to sleep, she dreamed of a mysterious Gypsy man with copper hair and ancient green eyes who threw her over his saddle with a lustful laugh and carried her off into the night...

"*Stop* sending me flowers!"

"Is that any way to say good morning?" Devon asked, wounded.

Tory stepped back to let him in the front door, gesturing wordlessly toward the living room. She found words, though, very aggrieved ones, and they followed him from the foyer. "Look. I appreciate the thought. I really do. However, not only is it costing you a fortune, not only have I become a joke to the delivery man, and not *only* have you sent the florist into creative fits by demanding a different bouquet every morning—but *I'm running out of room!*"

Devon didn't respond to her tirade until he got a good look at the latest floral offering, and then he burst out laughing.

It sat on the floor with a fascinated Whiskey staring at it, and it looked like nothing so much as a floral tribute a winning thoroughbred could expect. The red roses were shaped into a perfect horseshoe.

"Did I win the Kentucky Derby or what?" Tory wanted to know, staring at the offering.

Devon was still laughing. "Sorry. I knew the florist looked a bit ruffled when I told him I wanted something different, but I never thought his creative powers would be so limited."

"You can hardly blame the man; have you *counted* the arrangements you've had sent? Devon, please. Please stop sending the flowers."

"If you insist," he said woefully.

"I do." And when he instantly opened his mouth to speak, she neatly spiked his guns. "And, yes, I'll remember that phrase—*if* I ever have need of it."

"You will," he said, undaunted.

Wistfully, she said, "Once, just once, I'd love to

see you knocked off balance. I'd love to see you lose control."

"Be careful what you wish for." Devon's eyes went over her quite deliberately from her raven hair to her loafer-clad feet, taking in her snug jeans and gray cowl-neck sweater along the way. "You may get it."

Tory felt flushed and uncertain, and for one tremulous moment she very nearly caved in. Then the moment passed. Reluctantly, and leaving behind it tendrils of restless desire, but it passed. She reached desperately for normality and found it with a sudden responsibility.

"Oh, Phillip called. He tried his house first, but you must have already been on your way here. The number's by the phone; he said he needed to talk to you right away." She looked wryly at Devon. "He also said you'd called him shortly after meeting me and told him you needed his house for a while. He was very amused."

Devon didn't have the grace to look guilty, just cheerful. "Sure. I told him I'd met a knockout lady and planned to stick around."

"Uh-huh."

"Did Phillip say what he needed to talk to me about?" Devon was already reaching for the phone.

"Just something about a favor." Politely, Tory started to leave the room.

"Stay, please." He was dialing but spared a moment to raise an eyebrow at her. "I like looking at you."

Tory plucked Whiskey out of their favorite chair and sat down with him in her lap, sending Devon a halfhearted glare. Then she listened while he spoke to his brother.

"Phil? Yeah, I just got here. Of course not—although why you'd be calling your brother on your honeymoon—What? Well, no, I haven't even listened to the radio lately. Oh, that's funny. All right, get serious. Yeah. I see. Of course I will. Look, it's no problem; I still have Bobby's plane. I forgot you didn't know; it's a Lear, so there's no problem with the distance. Yeah. Hang on a minute, Phil."

The rather abstracted gaze Devon had fixed on Tory sharpened. "Honey, d'you have an atlas?"

"Sure." Tory went immediately to get it, bringing back a ruler as well, since she'd guessed what he needed. Her foresight won a quick smile and a kiss on her hand from him, and she retreated to her chair in some confusion, unsure whether it was the smile, the kiss, or his absent endearment that had shaken her.

Devon made some quick calculations with the map and ruler, then continued his conversation with his brother. "It's no problem, Phil. A bit over a thousand miles from Huntington to Bermuda, then about the same to Miami. Sure. I'll clear it with Bobby. Well, I don't know about that; I'll certainly try. Right. I'll call before I take off and give you an ETA."

He hung up and immediately placed a second call, still gazing at Tory. But his gaze was now more thoughtful than abstracted.

"Bobby. Listen, friend, when d'you need your plane back? I got distracted, and answer the question. That soon?" He did a few more calculations on the notepad by the phone, frowning slightly. "What?" No, no problem, it's just that I need to make a quick trip. Bermuda, then Miami and back. Phil needs to get to Miami, and there's some kind of snafu down there; he can't even charter a plane. Yeah. I think I can make it. Right. Hey—I owe you one. Okay, so I owe you a few! Bye."

Tory couldn't stand it anymore. "Who is Bobby?" she asked curiously.

'Hmm?" Devon's eyes laughed suddenly. "Well, he's a displaced Englishman whose family happened to make a fortune mining diamonds in South Africa."

After a moment of recalling certain newspaper and magazine articles, Tory voiced a small question. "Lord Robert? The playboy?"

Devon chuckled softly. "That's him."

Tory shook her head bemusedly, but Devon's next brisk question quickly recalled her attention.

"How would you like to take a little trip?"

She blinked. "A *little* trip?"

Devon was smiling, but his eyes were very intent. "Well, maybe not so little. I'm really being selfish in asking you, because it probably won't be a fun trip. We'll be in Bermuda and Miami just long enough to top off the tanks with fuel; I'll be fighting the clock all the way, since Bobby needs his plane soon. Phil and Angela will be aboard only to Miami; he has some business to take care of, and she's staying down there with him for the next couple of weeks."

Tory wondered briefly at Phillip's need to get to

Miami so quickly and at Devon's willingness to instantly fly to his rescue; they were obviously very close, but since she hardly knew what drove either man, it was useless to speculate.

In any case, a more immediate problem loomed.

"Devon, what about—"

"We can drop Whiskey off at Mrs. Jenkins's until we get back, although it won't really be long. We should make it back by late tonight, if you think you can cope with the tiring trip."

"It's not that. I just—"

"Please, *zingara?*"

There was a curious effect when Devon said *please,* Tory discovered somewhat grimly. His tone never altered, but the one simple word spoken by him caused her to instantly abandon her judgment, all objections, and her common sense. It did not bode well for her peace of mind.

"Devon, I—"

"Please?"

"Oh, hell."

Less than two hours later, Tory found herself buckled securely into the copilot's seat of a gleaming Lear jet, consciously willing herself to relax after the takeoff; it was the only part of flying she hated.

"That wasn't so bad, was it?" Devon asked cheerfully.

"Keep your eyes on the road," she directed instantly.

He laughed but complied; he was rather occupied

in any case by the demands of getting them to cruising altitude and on the correct heading. Tory watched him intently, gaining confidence from the ease with which he handled the duties of pilot. He was obviously expert and experienced at it, and she felt the last remaining bit of tension drain away.

The sound of the engines disturbed them very little in the cockpit, and once the jet had leveled off, she ventured a hesitant question. "What does your brother do for a living? I only met him briefly and haven't thought to ask since then."

Devon relaxed in his own seat, his eyes checking over dials and gauges with the automatic attention of someone who knew exactly what he was doing. "Phil's a corporate attorney. He played professional football for a few years after college—quarterback—then retired at a ridiculously young age to go to law school. The owner of his team tried every inducement you could name to get him to stay on, but Phil wasn't having any. He wanted to be a lawyer. Now he's one of the top corporate attorneys on the East Coast."

"And the trip to Miami?" she asked, still hesitant.

"Business. One of his clients has recently acquired some kind of company down there, and they're having legal problems. Phil has to straighten the situation out as soon as possible."

"I see." Tory glanced out to find only a thick blanket of cotton-candy clouds beneath them, then looked back at Devon. "He's older than you, isn't he?"

"Four years. Our sister—Jenny—is squarely in the middle. She's married and lives in Seattle."

"Are you an uncle?"

"Uh-huh. Niece and nephew."

Studying him silently, Tory wondered if this was quite the time to ask something she was reasonably sure would shake him off his balance. Being an artist, she was always interested in people. She had contained her curiosity about Devon's family until now; having sensed a faint reserve in him regarding one member of his family at least, she hadn't wanted to pry. But now her curiosity ate at her, because she very badly needed to understand the man Devon's life had shaped him into.

She took a deep breath. "Your parents?"

He answered casually. "My mother died when I was very young. My father's retired and lives in San Diego."

"And he ... didn't want you to become an archaeologist." It wasn't a question. When Devon's head turned sharply, his surprise was evident.

After a silent moment, he turned his eyes back to the "road." He seemed about to speak, then finally cleared his throat and said huskily, "A *very* perceptive lady."

Tory waited silently; he would talk about it or he wouldn't.

Devon stirred restlessly and made a few minor adjustments to the aircraft. When he began speaking, his voice was neither affable nor intense, but simply quiet. "My father is ... a very strong-willed man. He wanted certain things for his family—and from his family. He respects physical ability, a strong sense of competition . . . and winners. He always wanted to be an athlete himself; an injury sidelined him during his first year in college. The ambition never really died; years later, he just transferred it to his children.

"When Phil came along, he was the perfect son from our father's point of view. Athletic, competitive, and incredibly *good* at anything he turned his hand to. He enjoyed sports, but he wasn't driven the way our father was. In fact, I think he played pro football more to satisfy Dad than himself." Devon fell silent.

"And when you came along?" Tory questioned softly.

Automatically checking his instruments again, he continued wryly. "When I came along, I proved to be a major disappointment. Even when I was small, I was always more interested in looking at rocks than throwing them. Sports bored me. I didn't believe it was necessary to compete against anyone but myself. Dad . . . pushed."

His voice warming suddenly, Devon went on. "If it hadn't been for Phil, I don't think I'd have been able to stick it out as long as I did. He was a buffer between Dad and me. He defended my right to choose my own way and drew Dad's fire away from me time after time. And whenever Dad pointed to Phil's trophies and asked why I couldn't duplicate his achievements, Phil always stepped in to remind him that they were just symbols of fleeting moments, quickly forgotten, and that my scientific work would be remembered long after those trophies grew tarnished and dull.

"And I think Phil's decision to retire from pro football and pursue his own ambitions as an attorney helped me to go my own way."

Tory understood much better, now, why Devon had been so completely willing to fly to his brother's rescue. He was the kind of man who'd feel a debt after a childhood of Phillip's support and understanding. It was, she thought, a measure of his own strength and generosity of spirit that he had never hated the older brother who had clearly been the favorite son. Devon felt, instead, beholden to his brother for his support, and quite obviously loved Phillip very much.

She swallowed the aching lump in her throat, unwilling to question its existence. "What about your sister?" she managed.

Devon grinned just a little. "She very quietly and calmly decided to go her own way—and she did. No fuss, no bother. Jenny was a strong girl; she put herself through college. Phil and I helped when we could—and so did Dad, once he realized she knew what she was doing—but she did most of it on her own. She's a teacher now. History."

"Do you . . . see your father?"

"Oh, sure." His voice was ruefully affectionate. "We buried the hatchet years ago. He's still not terribly interested in my work, but I think he respects me for what I've achieved. We see each other several times a year, whenever the family gets together or when I get the chance to visit."

Tory stared at the clean lines of Devon's profile, thinking of her own father, the man she'd adored and respected intensely, and the lump rose again in her throat. Even though Devon and his father resolved their differences, she knew it couldn't have been easy for Devon. Without consciously willing the action, she reached out to touch his arm. "I'm sorry, Devon."

He looked at her, and it was as if a fleeting touch of gratitude had passed from him to her. Then he was smiling. "The past is past."

Soberly, Tory said, "No. It's like our shadows— always chasing after us."

"I suppose." He was still smiling, green eyes glowing warmly. "But I'm glad you decided to . . . stand in my shadow for a while. I'm glad you came along with me, *zingara*."

A course change demanded his attention, and Tory clasped her hands together in her lap and gazed blindly out at the cotton clouds.

Vulnerability. Chinks in the armor.

The father who had scorned his goals in life, who had belittled his chosen profession. A woman who had thought that same profession dull.

Tory thought of the complex man beside her who had bared at least a part of his soul to her, and she ached. Had it been the father, she wondered, who had unintentionally sparked such vast control in the son? A control necessary in deflecting scorn and ridicule? A control that rarely showed the intensity of a determined man hovering just beneath it?

She thought of the sensitivity of poetry and flowers and a kitten, of the humor that sharpened her wits and brought laughter bubbling to her throat. She thought of ancient green eyes and patient waiting.

And she thought that Devon had been right to warn her against wishing for something. She had gotten her wish: She had seen him off balance, seen the shadow of his past chasing after him. The chinks in his armor. More than that, though, she had seen him with different eyes, new eyes. Not the woman's eyes or the artist's, but a curious blend of both; for a fleeting moment, she had seen Devon as clearly as she ever would unless she painted him.

Unless she loved him.

Chapter 6

THEY WERE ON the ground in Bermuda for just slightly more than an hour; it took only that long to top off the fuel in the Lear's tanks and to get Phillip and Angela York safely aboard. Devon insisted that Tory stretch her legs while he went after his brother and sister-in-law, reminding her that they still had quite a trip in front of them.

She had brought her passport just in case, but no one asked to see it; she merely strolled around on the tarmac and watched the refueling procedures. Once back on board and after being reintroduced to Phillip and Angela, Tory was both amused and unsettled to realize that both had eyed her rather thoughtfully.

Amusement won out when Phillip, obviously lying through his teeth, announced that he and his wife were bored with each other's company; Angela immediately asked if she could ride up front with Devon, leaving Tory in the luxurious cabin with Phillip.

Tory waited until they were in the air and leveled off before loosening her seat belt and turning to him with a gentle smile, fully aware that the affection Devon felt for his brother was returned; Phillip quite clearly wanted to find out what kind of woman his brother was involved with. "You want to pump me now or wait awhile?" she asked dryly.

Phillip looked sheepish. "Is my curiosity that obvious?"

"Uh-huh." She smiled. "But nice, too. You really take care of your brother, don't you?"

"We take care of each other," he said firmly.

She studied him for a moment in silence. The similarity between them was unmistakable: They were much of a height; each had green eyes beneath batwing brows; each displayed a stubborn jaw and a determined chin. Phillip was dark, though, and his green eyes were more of an emerald color. And if he lacked that lurking, compelling intensity of his brother, he made up for it with sheer good-humored charm.

"I guess you got into the habit," she said finally, "with your father the way he was."

Phillip's eyes sharpened. "Devon told you about that?"

"Yes."

Whistling softly, he said, "That's a first."

Tory felt a bit uncomfortable beneath his scrutiny and tried to pass it off lightly. "That sounds like I'm the latest in a long line of ladies."

"No. Oh, no. That's never been Devon's way. He

makes friends hand over fist, but his work generally manages to keep him occupied. And then there was—" He broke off abruptly.

"Lisa," Tory said quietly.

"That, too," Phillip murmured, obviously referring to the fact that Devon had told her of Lisa. "Yes. She—she wasn't good for him. He realized that pretty quickly; my brother's no idiot. But it hurt. It left him wary. And I know he's damned tired of defending his way of life to those he cares about." He sighed. "Lisa thought his work was dull; she made no secret of that. And she was jealous of his complete dedication and of the time his work took him away from her. She was hardly the type to pack up a sleeping bag and go with him to some dig in the back of beyond!

"Other than that, as far as I know, their relationship was fine. Devon's work was the stumbling block." Phillip shrugged resignedly. "With Dad . . . well, things were harder because both Devon and Dad knew Devon was a born athlete."

Tory listened intently, realizing she would gain a slightly different perspective from Phillip. Devon had not spoken of himself as a "born athlete."

Phillip went on musingly, "He could handle any sport, but his heart wasn't in it. He never needed to be the fastest in track or the most valuable player in football or baseball. To Devon, sports were for exercise and fun—and Dad took the fun away. He even gave up karate—he studied it more for the discipline, I think—after earning a black belt, because Dad started pushing him to compete."

"Didn't your father realize how brilliant Devon is?"

Tory asked incredulously, unable to comprehend how anyone, particularly a parent, could ignore the vivid intelligence in those green eyes.

"That didn't matter," Phillip said simply. "Dad respects aggression and competitiveness over everything else."

Tory stirred restlessly. She didn't want to hear this; it made her ache inside. Ache for Devon. Childhood pains hurt the worst and the longest, and she ached now for a little boy who'd been unable to satisfy his father. And she didn't want to think about what her feeling that pain meant.

"But they get along now?"

"Oh, sure," Phillip said, sounding uncannily like his brother. "We're all adults now. In fact, the family ended up being pretty close, considering the distance between our respective homes."

She stared out the window.

"Tory?"

"Yes?" She looked at him, waiting.

He smiled a little crookedly, but his eyes were grave. "I know it sounds both impertinent and corny, but—"

"What are my intentions toward your brother?"

"Something like that."

Tory spoke slowly, searching for words. "Phillip, I—I don't want to hurt Devon. I certainly don't want him to defend his profession to me; I think it's fascinating work. Beyond that . . . I just don't know. You see, I'm wary, too."

Phillip didn't seem surprised. "I thought so. It's in your eyes."

She decided rather hastily that it was past time to lighten the conversation. "I don't think I like that," she commented with a frown.

He was nothing if not quick; he followed her lead instantly. "Wear dark glasses," he suggested gravely.

"I have a feeling that wouldn't be at all effective against the Yorks," Tory said definitely.

Phillip laughed and, as easily as that, they began talking about casual, unthreatening topics.

A few minutes later, Phillip went forward and traded places with his wife, who came back to sit with Tory.

Angela was a lovely brunette with sparkling brown eyes and a cheerful, irrepressible personality. Like Tory, she was a small woman, unlike Tory, she moved and spoke quickly. Collapsing into the seat beside Tory's with a long-suffering sigh, she said, "We should be in Miami before long—if Phil doesn't get us killed, that is."

Startled, Tory said, "He's flying the plane? Is he licensed?"

"Nope. He doesn't know the first thing about flying," Angela said cheerfully. "Devon's giving him instructions now. Let's hope they both pay attention to what they're doing."

Tory realized something abruptly. "Aren't we flying the edge of the Bermuda Triangle?"

The two women stared at each other for a moment.

Angela giggled a bit nervously. "I *hope,*" she said, "they're paying attention to what they're doing! And did you really have to say that just now?"

"Sorry. It popped into my head."

Angela looked at her with bright eyes. "Well, I'm sure neither of *them* believe in a Devil's Triangle. The question is, do either of *us* believe in it?"

"No," Tory said firmly after a moment's thought. "We don't believe in it, either."

"Oh, good. Then I can relax." Angela smiled at her. "So tell me. Have you thrown a rope around Devon yet?"

Prepared for the question or something similar, Tory remained unshaken. "Hardly."

"Has he thrown one around you?"

"No," Tory answered with more certainty than she felt.

"Uh-huh."

"Stop smiling at me, dammit."

"It's just that you sound so awfully sure. And so awfully familiar," Angela said apologetically.

"Familiar?"

"Mmm. Just the way I did—a few months ago."

"These York men," Tory muttered. "They were born to cause trouble."

"Isn't that the truth! And the worst of it is that they'd be hurt and horrified if we told them just how much trouble they cause."

Tory rested an elbow on the armrest, propping her chin in her hand and staring broodingly out the window. "At least with macho we knew where we stood," she said cryptically.

Angela giggled. "Right. Squarely behind the eight ball!"

Sending her new friend an amused look, Tory said,

"Okay, okay—three cheers for women's lib. It freed us. It freed them. We can be tough; they can be sensitive. Which leaves us with a nice round of confusion for all."

"And no game plan."

"Exactly. It took men and women two million years to establish clearly defined roles, and a single generation to wipe them out. Not, mind you, that I totally agree with those ancient roles, but—Look. Our grandmothers knew exactly what to expect from life; they might not have liked it, but they knew what roles were supposed to be theirs. Look at us. We're a generation on a guilt trip. We feel guilty if we have a career, guilty if we *don't* have a career, guilty if we have kids and can't live up to the Supermom image. Guilty if we *don't* have kids.

"We've been brainwashed by media hype and politics, and now we're torn between what we *think* we're supposed to be and what we feel we *want* to be. Our grandmothers looked for security in their men, but we're supposed to be secure in ourselves."

Tory blinked suddenly. "Hell. It must be jet lag coming on. Am I making sense?"

"No," Angela said politely. "But you rather neatly changed the subject. Or did you?"

Tory sighed. She looked at the other woman for a moment, sensing sympathy and an open hand of friendship, and she wasn't really surprised to hear her abstract confusion pouring out in specific detail.

"Maybe I didn't change the subject. It's not easy being a woman, is it? There are no rules anymore. I don't feel that I . . . fit in anywhere. I don't want to be the prototypical clinging vine, stuffed with emotion and basing all decisions on the way I feel. But I also don't want to be so—liberated—that I begin to believe I don't need anyone at all."

She smiled a little wryly. "I don't want to care for him, Angela, I really don't. I don't want to be vulnerable again. It isn't that I don't trust Devon; sometimes I think I trust him more than I trust myself. But I know that if I—if I let myself care for him, and it goes wrong somehow, I don't think I could stand it. I've gotten used to being alone. And I know that if I let him into my life, if I let myself care for him, nothing will ever be the same . . . and I'll have to learn to be alone all over again."

"Are you so sure you'd be alone?" Angela asked softly.

Tory gazed broodingly out the window. "Physically . . . maybe not. Maybe he'd stay, or want us to be together. But *emotionally* . . . I'd be alone. I don't know how to extend myself to him that way, and I'm afraid to try. Afraid he won't be there, or that he won't be what I think he is."

"The risk goes with the territory."

"Yes." Tory took a deep breath. "But I'm not sure I want to take that risk." She shook her head suddenly and sent a wry smile to her new friend. "It's amazing, isn't it? I mean, the convolutions we put our emotions through. Or is it just me?"

"Oh, no." Angela laughed ruefully. "D'you know, when I finally caved in and told Phil I loved him, I

was absolutely furious? I was crying and swearing—
in fact, I all but hit the man! He didn't know whether
to hold me or run wildly in the opposite direction."

"He obviously made the right choice."

"Well, I think so—although I wasn't too sure that
night!" Angela sobered abruptly. "You know, Tory,
it's all very well to talk about choices and whether or
not we want to care for someone, but in the end we
don't seem to have a lot of control in the matter. And
then, there's Devon; it's a risk for him, too. What if
he decides to take the risk and *you're* not there?"

At that moment, Phillip came into the cabin, spar-
ing Tory the necessity of answering Angela's question.
And she was glad, because she had no answer to give.

Phillip smiled cheerfully at Tory. "Devon wants
you up front—for luck, he says."

Tory rose to her feet, grateful when Angela asked
the question uppermost in her mind.

"What's wrong?" the other woman demanded instantly.

"Just a little rough weather coming up," Phillip
answered easily.

The two women looked at each other, and Angela
said mournfully, "The Devil's Triangle."

"Superstition," her husband told her firmly.

Angela frowned at him. "I hope somebody doesn't
find that written down years hence in a book of famous
last words."

Tory went hastily toward the cockpit, leaving the
couple to argue the point. She strapped herself into
the copilot's seat, sending Devon an anxious look.

"Should I have updated my will before we left?" she asked with forced lightness.

He smiled reassuringly. "We'll be fine. It looks worse than it'll feel to us, believe me."

For the first time, Tory glanced forward, and she bit back a gasp at what she saw. In the distance, far too close for comfort, reared an enormous thunderhead. The sun was completely hidden behind it, and lightning was flashing within it. It looked about as unfriendly as any type of weather possibly could.

Tory hesitantly voiced her worst fear. "That isn't a hurricane, I hope?"

"No, just a low-pressure area. Hell of it is, we can't get above it, and it's just too big to go around. Ergo, we fly through it."

"Great."

Devon smiled again. "Don't worry. I've been through worse."

"Yeah? When?" Tory was trying to keep her mind off the fast approaching storm.

"Last year," he replied instantly. "And in this jet, too. Bobby'd flown down to Central America, where I was working on a dig. When he decided to leave, he discovered that his pilot had come down with Montezuma's Revenge—or the Aztec Two-Step, if you prefer." Devon grinned at her. "Anyway, he asked me if I'd fly him home. It was fine with me, especially since a virtual monsoon was soaking the ruins."

"What happened?" Tory asked, wincing slightly as they began to enter the storm and rain lashed the jet viciously. "Or would you prefer to keep your mind on flying?" she added hastily.

"No problem," he said, laughing as he intercepted a doubtful glance from her. "Really. We're perfectly safe." He made a minor adjustment to their course, then said, "What happened? Well, about halfway over the Gulf, we had the misfortune to encounter last year's worst hurricane. If we'd thought to check the weather before taking off, we would have gone around the thing, but no one down there in the boonies offered to warn us. Anyway, we made it."

Tory was silent for a moment, nearly hypnotized by the eerie sight of lightning arcing in the surrounding clouds. The clouds themselves formed an almost smothering image of a dirty gray blanket wrapped around the jet, lanced with electricity and driving rain.

She fought to keep her voice level. "Bobby's interested in archaeology?"

"His hobby. He funds expeditions a couple of times a year."

"I meant to ask before"—Tory turned her head to look at him—"why Bobby's so generous with his plane."

"We're friends," Devon said.

Tory's gaze sharpened as she heard the touch of evasiveness in his voice, and she very nearly forgot the storm. "That isn't the whole reason, though, is it?" she guessed.

After a sidelong glance at her, Devon appeared to become fascinated by the instrument panel.

"Devon?"

He shifted his weight in obvious discomfort and

muttered, "You wouldn't believe me."

"Try me," she suggested, becoming more and more intrigued.

Sighing, he said, "Well, Bobby seems to think he owes me."

"Why?"

In the tone of one pushed inescapably into a corner, Devon said, "Because of a curse."

Tory blinked. "A curse?" She thought for a moment. "You mean, like the curse of King Tut's tomb?"

"Sort of. Aztec, though, not Egyptian."

Silently absorbing his very embarrassed tone, she swallowed a giggle. "I see."

"It's more of a joke than anything else," Devon said with rather heavy emphasis. "We don't actually *believe* in the curse, of course."

"Of course."

"Just a dumb joke."

"Uh-huh. Did you, uh, actually save him from this curse, or was it something more . . . nebulous?"

Devon sighed. "What I actually *did* was to keep him from being brained by a falling idol. Bobby decided I'd saved him from a curse. It's been a sort of running joke for years."

The jet shuddered just then, buffeted by strong winds as they entered the most violent part of the storm, and they dropped the subject of curses. It was almost as dark as night now, lightning flashing and thunder crashing even above the sound of the jet's engines.

While Devon was somewhat occupied with handling the craft, Tory suddenly remembered what the cards had predicted. "A storm," she murmured, more to herself than to him. "Danger."

Devon glanced over at her and, proving that he'd seen that little fortune-telling episode as something more than the joke she'd meant it to be, said, "Apparently you're more intuitive than you know."

Tory stirred uneasily. "Coincidence."

"Was it?" Devon studied her profile for a moment, then began speaking very deliberately. "I never thought much about intuition. I never thought it was something I'd ever feel myself; I suppose because I'm a scientist. But since I met you, I've been aware of . . . insights that have surprised me. Some of it, I suppose, can be explained rationally. Your paintings, for instance. What I saw in them could have been, perhaps, seen by anyone because of your sheer talent.

"But there've been other things, all of them connected to you. For instance, I've finally figured out why you're wary, Tory."

Tory knew what was expected of her, but she had to swallow before she could force the words out. "Oh? And why's that?"

"You don't trust your emotions. You don't trust your emotional *judgments*."

Highly conscious of the storm raging all around them, Tory wondered if the tension she felt could be attributed solely to the weather. "Emotion just clouds a—a situation."

Devon was silent for a moment; then he spoke softly. "Emotion is necessary, Tory. Without it, logic would be cold and rationality would be lifeless. D'you know the concept of yin and yang?"

She nodded. "Yes. It's symbolized by a circle with a curved line through it: One side is the passive, feminine; the other, the active, masculine."

"And it means," Devon said firmly, "that neither side is whole without the other. You should think about that, Tory. We were never meant to be either one or the other exclusively. I never realized I was intuitive until I met you. Perhaps you should begin to understand that you'll be . . . incomplete without your emotional, intuitive qualities."

Tory remained silent, but she was thinking about what he said. The storm raged on outside the plane, eerily beautiful and deadly, while her own personal storm raged within.

She was still thinking when they touched down in Miami, far beyond the storm.

Tory and Devon had dinner with the other couple— a rather hasty dinner since they were on a tight schedule—and then left the lights of the city behind as the Lear lifted up into the night.

Although she had thoroughly enjoyed the meal and the convivial conversation, Tory had been forced to make a determined effort not to lapse into long silences. She knew that the hours spent in the jet had something to do with it, but she also realized that her restlessness and abstraction couldn't entirely be blamed on anything other than herself.

Magda's gift of introspection made it impossible

for Tory to postpone her ruthless self-analysis; she was by nature one who would always question her own thoughts and emotions. But doing so this time brought her no closer to an answer.

Could she trust her emotional judgments? Was Devon right in believing that emotion and intuition were necessary? She had long believed that her work was based on some kind of science—on technique and logic—but had her own intuition played a larger part than she'd been willing to admit?

Could the answer really be that simple? Hadn't her image of Jordan been based on emotional judgment? And hadn't it taken the "science" of her art to prove the fallacy of that image? Or had she drawn on a deeper intuition that was, in fact, the basis of her art?

She stared out into darkness, aware that the man at her side sent her searching glances from time to time, aware of the faint light in the cockpit and the odd intimacy of being alone with him in darkness and so high above the earth. She sat perfectly still, remaining utterly silent as the truth rose up within her, drawn by his perception or unleashed by her own, too powerful to deny or ignore.

It was already too late. Too late for choices, for denials, for analysis. Too late for making a decision—any decision at all.

She was in love with Devon York.

"Tired?"

His voice came to her gently across the narrow space between them, and Tory turned her head to look at him. She felt, oddly, as if she were looking at him for the first time. Her voice, when it finally emerged, sounded normal to her. "A little."

"We'll be home soon," he said, still gentle.

Home.

Tory took a deep breath, attempting to disperse the fog that seemed to grip her mind so totally. It didn't do much good, she decided, but at least she was able to keep her voice level and calm. "Yes. I suppose it'd be better to wait until tomorrow to pick up Whiskey. I mean, since it'll be fairly late when we get back to the house."

"We'll get him tomorrow." Devon shot her another glance, wondering again what had happened to upset her. Although her voice and face both reflected calm, the fingers twisting together in her lap betrayed a restlessness he'd never seen in her before. And something in her eyes as she'd looked at him just then bothered him. *She looks so lost . . .*

He wanted to take her in his arms and comfort her, and he didn't stop to question why. She intrigued him, this tough lady with the strange Gypsy eyes and the wary soul. Her piquant face drew his eyes like a lodestone, and her very presence commanded his instant and total awareness.

Devon had never thought of himself as a patient man, and he saw no great virtue in the fact that he had not pressured her into a relationship she was clearly hesitant to begin. He was sure only that he wanted her to be as certain about her feelings as he was about his. And the desire he felt for her was a living thing inside him.

He looked at her again, feeling his body quicken in response, and then ruthlessly turned his attention to the craft he piloted. Time. They had time. And he meant to convince Tory Michaels that he belonged in her life—no matter how long that took.

Tory didn't think much during the remainder of the trip. She was in a kind of limbo and didn't try to disturb that. A sort of peace had come over her when she realized that she loved Devon, and she was content, for now, with that peace. In admitting the possibility of necessary emotion, she had given a name to her feelings.

They dropped the Lear at the airport in Huntington in the hands of the pilot Bobby had sent from D.C. to fetch it, then drove Phillip's truck up the winding mountain road to her house.

The silence between them had lasted too long to be comfortable; she knew Devon was puzzled by it, but she could find no words to explain to him. She could only invite him in for a drink and then stand in silence before the cold hearth in the living room as she sipped hers. And she was vaguely surprised to realize that he was restless and uneasy, pacing the room as if searching for something he couldn't find.

"I enjoyed the trip," she said finally.

"Good. I'm glad you went with me."

Silence again.

"Is something wrong?" he asked suddenly.

Tory glanced up to find him standing before her; then she looked back into her brandy. Inwardly acknowledging what she felt was one thing; she had no intention of voicing her feelings aloud. Not now. Not yet. "There's nothing wrong," she murmured.

"No?" He looked at her steadily, then deliberately eased off. "That's good. Listen, *zingara,* you're really going to have to marry me. Otherwise, my brother'll think you're toying with my affections."

She smiled just a little but still didn't look at him. "Remember Byron: 'When a man marries, dies, or turns Hindu, his best friends hear no more of him.' You wouldn't want that to happen."

"Byron was talking through his hat," Devon told her definitely. "The man was cynical and chronically bitter. And you evaded my proposal again."

Tory strove desperately for lightness and normality. "Well, I just don't know. You'd have to have several necessary qualities before I'd even *consider* marrying you."

"For instance?"

"Can you get a taxi in the rain?"

"Of course. Although it's not a very useful talent around here."

"Hmm. D'you like the window open or closed at night?"

"I'm flexible."

"I don't suppose you do windows?"

"In the spring and fall," he said instantly.

Tory tried to think of something else, something trivial and playful. But she couldn't. She was too stingingly aware of his lean body so close to her own, too aware of that damped-down pagan fire smoldering within her. And too aware of the fact that, teasing notwithstanding, his proposal-practicing now made her heart ache.

Words just wouldn't come.

When the deafening silence between them had stretched into minutes, Devon hesitated, then softly recited a verse from Lewis Carroll:

"'The time has come,' the Walrus said,
　'To talk of many things:
'Of shoes—and ships—and sealing wax—
　'Of cabbages—and kings—
'And why the sea is boiling hot—
'And whether pigs have wings.'"

Tory knew what he was saying. And she had come to know this man well enough to be sure he would not give up until he discovered why they had been saying meaningless things.

"Cards on the table," he said quietly. "What's wrong, *zingara?*"

Chapter 7

SHE REACHED UP to set her glass on the mantel, then looked at him finally, finding words that were inadequate but all she had. "I promised myself—after Jordan—that I wouldn't get involved again. The price is too high. It seemed to me that turning two people into . . . emotional punching bags for each other was just insanity."

"It doesn't have to be that way," Devon objected firmly.

"No?" Tory smiled a little wryly, aware that the long day and the rawness of her emotions had left her vulnerable. "Maybe not. But the risk . . . I need my emotional energy, Devon. Contrary to popular opinion, suffering doesn't make an artist great; an unhappy artist is no more productive than an unhappy individual in any line of work. And I have to paint. D'you understand that? I *have* to."

Devon nodded slowly. "I understand that. And I understand that you've been hurt, and that you're wary." His face was very still, the vivid green eyes direct and honest. "But, Tory, I don't believe I'd be bad for you. God knows I can't be very objective about that, but I honestly believe you need me as much as I need you. And I can't walk away from that. Give me a chance, *zingara*. Give us a chance."

"I thought that's what I'd been doing," she managed unsteadily.

"And?" he questioned quietly, setting his glass on the mantel.

Tory swallowed hard, then said starkly, "I hate it when you leave me, and I hate myself for feeling that way. Dammit, I'm getting involved again, and I don't want to!"

"Shh." He reached out abruptly, pulling her into his arms and holding her tightly. "You're tired—"

"I'm tired of being alone," she said huskily, her arms slipping around his waist of their own volition. "I'd gotten used to it, and then you came along, and now I can't stand it anymore."

"Tory . . ."

"Stay with me," she whispered almost inaudibly.

Devon went still for a moment, then drew away just far enough to turn her face up and gaze into gray eyes gone a smoky violet. "If only I could be sure you know what you're doing," he breathed.

"Don't you understand?" She conjured a small, crooked smile from somewhere. "That's the problem:

I know exactly what I'm doing."

He stared at her for a moment, then said fiercely, "I won't hurt you!"

"Then don't leave me."

"Tory..."

His hesitation, oddly enough, sealed her own decision; his control sent hers winging into oblivion. The only thing she was sure of was that she wanted this night with him. She wanted all the nights she could hold in her mind and in her heart. And if some tomorrow demanded a price of her, she would pay it—tomorrow. Tory threw her love and her fate into the laps of the gods. She turned her face, touching her lips to his wrist and feeling the tiny pulse there beating wildly. "Please stay."

Devon's breath caught harshly in his throat, and his green eyes blazed with a savagery that showed only there. Hands still framing her face, he bent his head slowly until his lips gently teased hers apart. His breath becoming hers, he whispered, "I need you... God, how I need you... if you're sure, Tory..."

Her arms moved to encircle his neck, her fingers toying briefly with his golden earring. "I'm sure," she murmured, molding her body to his and feeling her senses beginning to whirl.

His mouth slanted across hers, driving, possessive, as if he would take everything she had to give and still need more. It became almost a battle as they fenced with living blades, an explosion of desire more powerful than either of them had expected.

Tory clung to him as he swept her up into his arms,

her fingers locked in his hair. She knew he was carrying her up the stairs to her bedroom, and she felt oddly cherished being held in his arms as easily as if she were a child. But the feelings inside her were hardly those of a child.

Devon set her gently on her feet beside her wide bed, bending to fling back the covers and turn on the lamp on the nightstand. A soft golden light spilled over the bed and over them, leaving the room's corners shadowed and isolating them in intimacy. He lifted his hands again, holding her face as his lips rained warm kisses over her closed eyes, her cheeks, her brow. Tory's fingers pushed the jacket from his shoulders and, as he shrugged it to the floor, searched out the buttons of his shirt.

It had become impossible to breathe, yet Tory scarcely even noticed. Her sweater was tossed aside; she couldn't remember if he had removed it or if she had. His shirt fell to the floor as she stepped out of her shoes and kicked them aside. Clothing lay where it fell, neither of them caring.

Hands spanning her narrow waist, Devon drew her forward slowly, his lips feathering lightly down her throat and past her collarbone, tracing the lacy border of her bra to the shadowed valley between her breasts. What little breath Tory could command caught in her throat, her body shivering beneath his touch. She felt her jeans sliding over her hips, and then he was lifting her easily and placing her on the bed.

Reluctant to lose his touch for even a moment, Tory forced her arms to release him, lying back on the pillows and watching him with passion-drugged eyes as he flung aside the remainder of his clothing. He symbolized the pagan fire in her blood, the hard planes and angles of his lean, powerful body riveting in the lamplight. He was as handsome as a blooded stallion and twice as dangerous, and she wondered dizzily why on earth she had waited so long for this night.

He came down on the bed beside her, accepting the silent invitation of her open arms with a low, husky groan. Shaking hands smoothed away her delicate underthings and then stroked fire into her awakened flesh as his vivid green eyes raked her body hungrily.

"Oh, God, you're beautiful," he said raggedly, his hot breath drawing a throbbing need from some core within her even before his lips touched her.

Tory bit her lip on a gasp, her hands gripping his shoulders fiercely. Ripples of fire scalded her body, burning her nerve endings raw as his avid mouth surrounded the pointed need of her breast. Her heart thudded beneath his caress, expanded, pounded in her ears. She held on to him, almost afraid because he seemed the only reality in a world teetering on the brink of madness.

She could never afterward pinpoint exactly when the devil was born inside her, but somehow it sprang into life. A feminine devil, a fire-devil, it took hold of her mind with a relentless grip and released a molten passion as old as the cave. And it freed her in some mysterious way, loosening the restraints of hesitation, doubt, and shyness. She became something she had never been before, something primitive, and the craving in her body and mind drove her recklessly.

And Devon's control couldn't stand against the onslaught.

Her hands and lips explored his body feverishly, learning him in a way she'd never known a man before. She went a little crazy, submerging herself in this new discovery, this enchantment of the senses. Her caresses drew hoarse groans from his throat and shudders from his body, his whispered encouragements growing strained and finally frantic. And still she teased and incited.

The bulk of physical power lay easily with Devon, but it was her fire-devil that finally snapped his control and drove him over the edge.

The storm erupted with all the force of nature's fury, pulling them into a crucible's white blaze. They moved with the grace of dancers and the lethal power of jungle predators, loving and warring with an intensity only a breath away from madness.

And then there was only that, only madness, and only each other to cling to. They cried out with one voice in torment, in delight as the crucible finally released them . . . tested in the fire and not found wanting.

Exhausted, drained of everything save incredulity, they lay entwined on the lamplit bed. As if a massive earthquake had shaken them, aftershocks continued to send tremors through their bodies. Devon had drawn the covers up over them, and he held Tory close to his side as if in fear of losing her somehow, almost compulsively stroking her hair and the arm that lay across his chest.

"My God," he murmured at last.

Tory rubbed her cheek against his shoulder, still stunned and wide awake. She didn't know what had happened between them, but she had never felt so close to another human being in her life.

"You are . . . something else, *zingara*."

"You're not so bad yourself," she said huskily, reaching for airiness because she couldn't handle anything else in that moment.

Devon followed her lead instantly. "I hope you'll respect me in the morning," he said, anxious.

She giggled. "I always knew you were easy."

"I guess that's why you threw yourself at me."

"Obviously."

"You were carrying coals to Newcastle, you know."

"You're amorous by habit, huh?"

"By nature, actually. Just call me Lothario."

"Hmm. What does that make me?"

"That's a loaded question."

"Funny."

"Well. You're my conquest."

"Oh? You should never confuse women with trophies."

"Was I doing that?"

"Definitely."

"Sorry. Then you can be my consort."

"Only if you're a prince or a king."

"Am I not?"

"No. You're my shining knight."

"Right. Your shining knight on a donkey."

"Whatever works."

He hugged her suddenly. "And you're my angel. Even if you *don't* have a halo."

"Halo?" She reached toward her head and felt around. "Damn—it's gone. Did you steal my halo?"

"Well, I needed a souvenir."

"Give it back."

"No way. It's hard enough to cope with a 'bright, particular star' without worrying about hanging on to a halo-bearing angel."

Tory giggled suddenly. "Uncle! The honors go to you. I think faster vertically and clothed."

"You're no slouch horizontally and unclothed, let me tell you."

"Devon!"

"Thinking. I meant thinking."

"Uh-huh."

"Really. Of course, you're also exceptionally good—"

"I'll take it as read," she interrupted firmly.

He chuckled. "Ambiguous phrases."

"The whole conversation's lousy with them."

"Then how about an explicit statement?"

"What?" she asked guardedly.

"It's raining."

Tory started laughing.

"Got you, didn't I?" Devon was clearly satisfied.

"I should learn not to try to guess what you're

thinking," she responded, resigned.

"Guess what I'm thinking now."

She gasped and murmured rather uncertainly, "You—um—aren't you tired?"

"Not that tired," he said huskily, smoothly shifting position until he was propped up on an elbow beside her. His hand continued to move seductively over golden flesh, and his lips began to probe her jawline. "How about you?"

Tory didn't bother to answer. Not with words.

Quite some time later, Devon reached out a long arm to turn off the lamp. *"Exceptionally* good," he noted in a drained, sleepy voice.

Tory smiled drowsily, lying securely close to his side, the steady sound of his heart beating beneath her ear lulling her to sleep.

Tory knew she was awake, but, like every morning, she resisted opening her eyes until the last possible moment. Only the rather abrupt awareness that Devon was awake finally prompted her to stir; he was stroking her hair very lightly and, if her hazy memories of the night were correct, she realized neither of them had budged an inch in sleep.

She moved very slightly and felt the instant response of his arm tightening around her. "You're a snuggler, aren't you?" Her voice, heavy with sleep and amusement, was muffled against the tanned flesh of his throat.

"I'm a what?"

"A snuggler. Someone who snuggles. In bed. I've never slept with a snuggler before."

"Good." He tilted her chin up, kissing her softly. "Good morning."

Tory gazed into impossibly green eyes, thinking vaguely that it must have been weariness that had caused her to act the way she had last night. God, had that really been she? That wanton woman? She felt heat suffuse her throat and steal up her face.

Devon chuckled softly. "Don't look so horrified, *zingara;* you'll hurt my feelings if you wake up every morning wearing that expression!"

"It's not that," she denied almost inaudibly. "It's just that I—that I've never—"

"You've never—?" he prompted softly.

"Felt that way before."

"Neither have I."

She looked at him a little shyly. "No?"

"No." He traced the curve of her lips with a gentle finger. "Together we make magic, tough lady."

Tory laughed shakily. "The cards were right."

Devon's fallen-angel smile lit his eyes. "I hate to say I told you so, but—"

"But you can't resist!"

"It's a quirk in my character," he explained apologetically.

"You seem to have a lot of those."

"I beg your pardon."

"You do. Insatiable curiosity, the patience of Job, a nutty sense of humor, and the control of a saint."

"Those don't sound like quirks."

"They are. They don't—they don't mesh." She was only half teasing, her mind still puzzled by the complex, conflicting qualities of this man.

"Look who's talking."

"I don't conflict," she stated in surprise.

He started laughing, a soft, rueful sound. "Oh no? Sweetheart, as far as I'm concerned, you're the most fascinating mystery since Stonehenge."

"I am?" Her voice was blank.

"Definitely. And it just might be worth the rest of my life to eventually figure you out."

A part of Tory wanted to ask him to explain that remark, but a larger part just wasn't ready for even an elusive verbal commitment. Besides, Devon seemed to be having no problems with energy this morning, and somehow or another, she forgot to ask him anything at all . . .

They shared a shower when they found the strength for it, then went downstairs, where Devon once again demonstrated his ability to prepare breakfast and keep her giggling at the same time. And Tory found, somewhat to her surprise, that mornings were really enjoyable with the right company.

Nobly insisting on doing her share by cleaning up, Tory restored the kitchen to order while Devon went to pick up Whiskey from Mrs. Jenkins. She finished some time before he returned, and, feeling the long overdue itch in her mind and fingers, fetched her sketchpad from the workroom.

It was a warm and sunny day, a sample of Indian summer, and fresh air beckoned. She threw open the French doors and stepped out onto the patio, looking at the view of rolling mountains and valleys that had originally sold her on this house. Making use of one of the redwood lounge chairs Angela had left with the house, Tory sat down and propped the sketchpad on her upraised knees. She stuck one charcoal pencil into the accustomed spot above her right ear and used a second pencil to begin shaping a mountain on paper.

She stopped, the sketch incomplete, only moments later. Something nagged at her, tickled like a feather in her mind. She stared at the paper mountain, battling silently, then gave in with a quick sigh.

Only the first step, she assured herself resolutely. There was no danger in that, no danger in committing to paper the qualities she saw in him. The first step never revealed much, after all, just surface appearance and perhaps a trick of expression.

The first step . . .

Turning the heavy paper, she abandoned the mountain, and smoky lines and curves began to appear on the clean page. Slowly at first, jerky with reluctance, her movements gradually smoothed and quickened. She sketched entirely from her mind's eye, staring fixedly at the emerging portrait.

The man had broad shoulders, his head well and proudly set on a strong neck. His thick hair was a little windblown, his head tilted ever so slightly to one side. A faint smile curved his rather hard mouth, revealing humor but something else as well, something elusive.

Tory closed her mind to all things elusive and went on sketching.

High, well-formed cheekbones. The nose just a bit crooked, the jaw stubborn. Flying brows. Eyes... eyes that were strikingly, vividly *alive* in the lean face, and very direct.

She stared down at the likeness of Devon for a long moment, then slowly closed the pad. Hugging it to her breast, she gazed out over the mountains, unseeing. "There's beautiful scenery," she murmured to herself, not even seeing it. "And all the heirlooms for still lifes. There's Whiskey. I don't *need* to paint you, Devon. I'll just... I'll just enjoy you for as long as you stay with me. If you leave—*when* you leave, I'll paint you. It won't matter if it hurts then."

And it just might be worth the rest of my life to eventually figure you out.

"Ambiguous," she muttered as the memory of his words rose to her mind. "He could have meant anything."

The sound of the truck pulling up near the house yanked her from thought, and she immediately rose and went inside, closing the French doors behind her. She slid the sketchpad and pencils into the drawer of the corner table, turning away just as Devon entered the room.

"Your cat," he announced dryly, "very nearly caused a major pileup a little while ago. He *would* try to climb onto my shoulder while I was driving." He handed her the maligned feline, adding firmly, "We'll get him a carrier."

"Don't *you* like to see where you're going?" Tory defended, scratching behind Whiskey's outsize ears in welcome before setting him on the floor and watching him scamper off toward the kitchen.

"I," Devon responded unanswerably, "am not a cat."

Tory started to tell him that he walked like one, but she bit back the words. She reminded herself fiercely to keep things easy, but before she could follow through he had reached out abruptly and hugged her. Hard.

Returning the hug with interest, she smiled up at him. "What was that for?"

He shook his head slightly, as though puzzled by his own action, and said a bit gruffly, "You look so lost in the morning."

"It's afternoon," she pointed out lightly.

"Yes, but you're still wearing your lost look."

"I have this system for facing the day," she explained solemnly.

"Which is?"

"I delay it as long as possible. Then I stagger around doing my impersonation of a zombie for a while. Then I drown myself in coffee. Somewhere in all that, the day becomes reality for me."

He lifted a quizzical brow. "I don't recall you staggering this morning."

"That's because I was leaning on you."

"And after I left, you backslid?"

"Exactly."

"You need a keeper."

"Not at all." Tory slipped out of his arms and went to sit on the couch. "What I really need are some answers."

"To which questions?" he asked politely, joining her on the couch.

Intending both to satisfy her curiosity and to keep things light, she said, "Well, I've been wondering. I know what an archaeologist *does,* but what I don't know is how you make a living at it. D'you teach? D'you have a grant or work for a museum?"

"All of the above. I'm a consultant for a museum in D.C. at the moment. And I'll begin teaching again this winter at a nearby university."

"Nearby in D.C.?"

"Nope. Nearby here."

She tried not to think of Devon being so near if their relationship didn't last. "So no more desert?"

"Not for a while. I usually spend a few months a year at a dig." He was smiling at her, adding innocently, "Lots of interesting subjects for an artist at a dig."

"I'm sure."

"Really. Just think of it. Beautiful sunsets. The wind whining through the ruins of an ancient civilization. Pieces of the past."

"Right," she said noncommittally. "But I still have

questions. So tell me about your work."

Apparently realizing that she was honestly interested, he did. He told her about past digs, enlivening the details of methodical work with descriptions of people he'd met and fascinating places he'd seen. He talked seriously about some lasting impressions he'd gotten, such as of the Sahara: "A beautiful, haunting, dying land." And cheerfully about other impressions: "You should ride a camel; it's an experience not to be missed. I've never felt more insignificant in my life than when one of the creatures stared at me. Talk about daunting!"

He told her about sandstorms and flash floods, boiling days and freezing nights. About the patient sifting of dirt and the labor of digging down through layers of time.

Tory was fascinated, keeping him talking by asking questions and listening intently. They gravitated to the kitchen later to prepare a late lunch, the conversation branching off along various similar paths. Tory had seen many of the world's major cities, having studied art in Paris and traveled with her father, and she now contributed her own observations and impressions.

They were more relaxed with each other than they had ever been, and when the conversation—and everything else—abruptly changed, it caught Tory completely unaware. She had her back to Devon and was tossing the salad while he was across the room turning steaks beneath the broiler.

"Marry me," he said suddenly.

Tory was already turning toward him, one of the quotations she'd memorized on the tip of her tongue, when the hoarseness of his voice struck her. She looked at him, her smile fading, seeing an odd, solemn alarm on his face, and feeling her heart lurch.

"You're serious," she whispered.

He nodded jerkily. "I'm serious. Odd, when I finally proposed for real, I could only think of the words. All that practicing shot to hell."

Chapter 8

TORY WAS NEITHER controlled enough nor insensitive enough to respond lightly, especially when she could see how shaken he was by his own words. And she couldn't sort out her own tangled emotions enough to make sense of them. But one thing was clear: She had to make him understand the fear she barely understood herself.

"I want to show you something," she said finally.

Devon looked at her for a long moment, apparently realizing that she was not changing the subject, then nodded. "All right."

She turned off the oven, then led the way to her workroom. Devon had not been in the room since that first day; Tory had unpacked the remainder of her finished canvases and arranged her equipment and supplies herself. She said nothing when they entered

127

the room, but merely pointed to one corner, where the sunlight slanting through the uncurtained windows shone brightly on canvases leaning against the walls.

Devon hesitated only briefly before approaching the paintings. "Is this my answer?" he asked quietly, gazing at her.

"In a way." She took a deep breath. "I can't think about marriage, Devon. Not now."

"Marriage? Or marrying me?"

"Both."

He leaned a shoulder against the wall, sliding his hands into the pockets of his slacks and continuing to stare at her. He ignored the paintings. "What about last night?" he asked tersely.

Tory knew he was disturbed and confused; she wanted to run to him, cling to him, tell him she loved him. She wanted to respond to the vulnerability she saw so clearly in his remarkable eyes.

But that final blowup with Jordan haunted her. Her bewilderment and despair, his vicious lashing-out because of her belated honesty. The pain of losing a love that had never really been hers.

Devon wasn't Jordan; he could never, she was sure, lash out at anyone in viciousness or cruelty. But still Tory resisted the commitment of three small words and an open heart. She had a choice to make first, a choice between two potential heartaches: Paint Devon now and discover if what she felt for him was real, or allow her love for him to become even more deeply embedded in her heart before being forced to paint him.

Either way, she risked the agony of losing a love

that was already far more important to her than Jordan's had ever been.

"You know what last night meant to me," she said finally.

"I thought I did. It looks like I was wrong."

Tory almost reached out to him then, responding instantly to the thinly veiled pain in his voice. But her fingers twined together in front of her, and her feet remained rooted to the floor. "No. No, you weren't wrong," she said unsteadily.

"Then why won't you marry me?" he asked, adding fiercely, "I said I'd never hurt you, Tory, and I meant it."

"I know. I know that. Please, Devon, can't we just let things go on the way they are?"

"Why?" he asked flatly.

"Because I need . . . time."

"I thought we'd gotten past that."

She had no answer, or at least no answer she thought he'd understand. And she tried desperately to lighten the moment. "Just my luck to find the only man around who *wants* strings."

He didn't smile. "And rings, and promises. I was never looking for an affair, Tory."

"You weren't looking for marriage, either."

"Not consciously when I knocked on your door that first morning. Maybe not even when I was— practicing proposals. But I think that in essence I was. I think I've always wanted to marry you."

She fell back on the practical, the sensible. "You don't know me."

"I'm *learning* you, Tory; I'll know you if you'll

only give me the chance."

"You see? We need time."

He stared at her for a long moment, and then his face tightened almost imperceptibly. "Well, let that be a lesson to me," he said evenly. "I guess that, like the boy who cried wolf, I proposed one time too many."

Tory took a jerky step toward him and stopped. "Devon, you're a part of my life." She tried to keep her voice steady and knew that she failed. "I'd—miss you terribly if you left me. But right now I don't know what I'm feeling, and I can't seem to think very clearly. All I know is that I can't . . . make another mistake. The last one cost me too much. I have to be *sure*. Can you understand that?"

Abruptly, Devon's stiff pose relaxed, and he came swiftly across to draw her into his arms. He was no longer the taut stranger who had very nearly frightened her. "I'm sorry, sweetheart," he breathed huskily. "I'm sorry. I was rushing you—and after I promised not to. Don't cry, *zingara*—I can take anything but that."

To her vague surprise, Tory realized that she *was* crying. She slipped her arms around his waist and held on tightly, burying her face in the smooth fabric covering his shoulder. "Tough ladies don't cry," she said with watery humor, her voice a little muffled.

"That's what I thought," he chided gently. "It looks like neither one of us is batting a thousand today."

"It's just training camp," she explained, finally lifting her head to smile uncertainly up at him. "We'll do better during the season."

"I hope so," he said wryly, reaching for a handkerchief to dry her cheeks. "We could hardly do worse."

"Oh, I don't know," she murmured, memories of the night before rising in her mind. "We've gotten some things right."

Devon's eyes darkened, his thoughts apparently running on the same track as hers. "We certainly have," he said, kissing her with a sudden fierce passion.

Tory lost her breath somewhere during the interlude and didn't really care. She threaded her fingers among the copper strands of his hair, her mouth blooming beneath his, only dimly aware that her fire-devil was etching yet another brand of possession.

"You and your ancient eyes," she managed after regaining her breath.

"My what?" he asked, smiling quizzically, his green eyes still dark and compelling.

"Ancient eyes. Gypsy eyes."

"You're the one with the strange Gypsy eyes, *zingara*," he murmured.

Tory, her fingers idly toying with the almost invisible earring, smiled suddenly. "No, you're the Gypsy. Ancient eyes and a golden earring and the charm of Lucifer himself."

Her mention of the earring brought a sheepish expression to his lean face. "Hell, I forgot the thing again. Would you mind taking it out for me?"

"Yes, I would mind. I like it."

"Tory—"

"Besides"—Tory choked back a giggle as her exploring fingers discovered something else—"you don't seem to have a choice at the moment. I don't have anything small enough to cut it."

"What?"

"Well, didn't you notice anything about it when they put it in?"

"All I noticed," he said definitely, "was that it hurt. Why d'you need something small enough to cut it?"

"Because it's a sealed loop, Devon. And part of that pain you remember may have occurred when they used heat to solder it."

"Dammit!"

"Maybe you'd better forget it again," she suggested.

He sighed. "I suppose I could find a discreet jeweler?"

"Good luck."

"Ah, hell."

"And, you know, even if a jeweler cuts it, the edges are going to be ragged; it'll probably hurt to take it out."

"You cheer me up any more," he said, deadpan, "and I'm not going to be able to stand it."

"Sorry."

"I am not," he muttered, "going to be very popular in certain places wearing an earring."

"You'll be *very* popular in other places, though." He stared at her.

"Native tribes and such," she clarified innocently.

"Uh-huh."

"And if you're invited to any masquerade parties, you have at least two choices of costume now: Gypsy or pirate."

"Tory..." he began dangerously.

"I'm only trying to help."

"Stop trying to help. Please."

"Well, I think it's cute."

Devon winced. "Why don't you just shoot me and put me out of my misery?" he suggested mournfully.

She hugged him. "I have so much fun when I'm with you."

"Good." He grinned. "I'm glad I'm useful for something."

"Fishing?" she asked.

"I'm not too proud. And just as soon as I find the right bait, I'll catch you, tough lady."

"Coming from a liberated man, that sounds suspiciously like treason," she observed thoughtfully.

"Am I liberated?"

"Certainly. Men can be sensitive, and women can be tough. And one day it'll work out nicely."

"But not now?"

"Things are a little confused. You may have noticed."

"I thought it was just me."

She giggled at his wistful tone. "Hardly. We're all confused."

"Oh. Well, my planning to 'catch' you may sound like treason, but it doesn't stop the plan. I'm going to make myself indispensable to you, *zingara*. One way or another."

"You don't have far to go," she said honestly, and then abruptly remembered something. "You called me something else once," she said slowly. "Not *zingara*, but something else."

Devon nodded immediately. "Tzigane. It means Gypsy. In French it's *gitane.*"

"D'you speak Italian and French?"

"Nope."

Tory smiled just a little. "Odd that you know those words, then."

He was smiling, too. "Not odd at all. Fate always intended me to fall for a Gypsy."

"Seriously. How do you happen to know so many words for Gypsy?"

His smile fading to something elusive, he murmured, "You'll think it's weird."

"So what else is new?"

"Funny."

"Okay, okay. Just tell me."

"I don't remember."

"What?"

"I don't remember how or why I know the words. I just know."

"That's weird."

"Uh-huh."

Tory stared at him. "I mean, really weird. Like the cards that night." She frowned. "I sense your fine hand in this somehow."

"I could hardly have stacked the deck when you were fortune-telling," he observed reasonably. "You handled the cards."

Tory conceded the point reluctantly. "True. But those words—"

"I swear, solemnly swear, on my *honor* that I can't

remember when or how or why I learned the words."

"Devon, this is definitely weird."

"Fate."

She stared at him, suspicious but shaken nonetheless.

"Didn't you want me to look at those paintings?" he asked idly.

Tory nodded slowly.

"Shall I?"

"Please." She watched him begin examining the paintings, and then, frowning, she left the room. Returning moments later, she announced calmly, "They're real. The words. I looked them up. French and Italian, and they both mean Gypsy. Are you *sure* you didn't look them up after we met?"

"I'm sure," he answered absently, obviously intent on studying the paintings.

Tory shook her head bemusedly and leaned against a table holding jars of brushes and tubes of paint, watching him. The sunlight caught him in a golden halo, the earring he wore reflecting a brilliant pinpoint of light from time to time, throwing a sudden shower of sparks as he moved suddenly. It suited him, she thought. Then she frowned as she stopped to turn her mind over, vaguely noticing something underneath it.

Her father's deep voice swam up through memory, cheerfully reciting something he'd heard at Magda's knee, something the Gypsies believed in above all else and never questioned.

"If your true love wears a golden earring, then he belongs to you."

She bit her lip and stared at Devon, realizing that it was too late, that it had always been too late to spare herself potential pain. He belonged with her. He belonged to her—even as she belonged to him. Emotional judgment or not, the feeling was too powerful to ignore.

In novels, Tory knew, the "point of no return" was often discussed at great length and suitably shadowed with pretty words. It was important in that a corner had been reached by the characters who traveled a suddenly one-way corridor. No going back. "Unto the breach, dear friends..."

And in a love story, the heroine would be wide-eyed, possibly tearful, and suddenly consumed by the realization that she was fathoms deep in love and couldn't swim, poor dear. She would gaze at the hero with hungry eyes and promptly sink all her scruples, abandon all her principles, and dissolve willingly into the raptures of love.

It didn't happen like that with Tory.

She watched as he repeated the gesture that had inexplicably stopped her heart, a ridiculously common gesture seen anywhere. Long brown fingers raked through copper hair. Restlessly, abstractedly, creating attractive disorder out of attractive order. He was a big man, loose-limbed, powerful but slim. His copper hair shone like a beacon. His face was strong and somewhat arrogant, with a nose that had been broken at least once and possibly more than once. His jaw bordered on the stubborn; his mouth was hard and yet possessed sensuality and humor and an elusive something else within its slight curve; russet bat-wing brows provided a strangely touching symmetry for his rough face.

Detached, somehow distant from herself, Tory studied him. As if, she thought vaguely, that other artist, the one who had made him, had decided to carefully contrast the finished and the incomplete. The hard face, with its crooked nose and stubborn jaw, was not yet finished. It would acquire lines of time and character, grow leaner with passing years. But his brows, she somehow knew, had been perfect from birth.

And Tory knew, in that moment, what was happening to her, and she acknowledged it completely and finally. She was perfectly still and utterly silent, listening for the sounds of scruples sinking and principles abandoned, waiting for the rapture that didn't show itself with a hint or a whisper.

Was it like that, then? she wondered. She was still herself, with scruples and principles intact, but raw and oddly untried.

You know how to swim, she reminded herself firmly. You've been in over your head before, and you survived. You made it to the shore and, dammit, you pulled yourself out!

Tory looked down at her hands as if she'd never seen them before, spreading the long fingers, studying a smudge of charcoal marring one knuckle. And wondered, defeated, when she would paint—try to paint him.

She looked back at him. He was studying the paintings, paintings of people rather than places or things. Precious few of them. They were mostly of women and children, with a smattering of men she'd asked to pose for her because of their interesting faces. Old men. Two of her character studies were missing, although, of course, Devon had no way of knowing that. The painting of her father, done entirely from memory, was on loan at the moment to a gallery in New York where his very first showing had been held.

The portrait of Jordan was still crated and stood in a corner, untouched.

Devon turned from the last painting, one of an old man with the dignity of years and cares on his face, and gazed at her, his eyes bright. "D'you accept commissions?"

She nodded.

"Would you accept one from me?"

She looked at him and said very softly, "I won't paint you." And her voice had the sound of a whisper that wanted to be a scream, a shriek of protest against what had to be.

"Am I unpaintable?" he asked with comical seriousness.

Tory didn't laugh. She half turned away from him. "You're . . . eminently paintable," she said, realizing in her distant observation of herself that her voice had gone somewhere else.

Devon crossed the room to her, and as she looked unwillingly up at him, she saw again that he was a perceptive man—or that she looked like hell.

"Something's hurt you," he said abruptly, the per-

fect bat-wing brows drawing together and his big body
tensing as if preparing to do battle.

Tory did laugh then, a soft, almost soundless laugh
that would do, she thought, as a substitute for tears.
"I won't paint you," she repeated, gazing up at the
finished brows and the unfinished face and the eyes
that were worried for her.

He frowned harder. Large hands rose to rest on her
shoulders. "What is it?" he asked in a new voice.
"What's wrong?"

She lowered her gaze to the third button of his
shirt, studying with the fixed stare of memorizing.
Russet hair, because the first two buttons were un-
fastened. Tanned flesh beneath. Hard muscle beneath
that. A heart beating somewhere beneath that, beating
with strength and force and certainty. "I . . . need to
be alone, Devon," she said, and his name echoed in
her ears and her mind.

He was silent for a moment; then his hands tightened gently. "I can't leave you," he said. "Not when
you're like this. Not when I don't understand what's
happened."

He won't even let me drown decently.

"I need to be alone," she repeated steadily.

"Look at me," he commanded, oddly rough.

"I need to be alone." She felt like a character from
a grade-B movie.

"Tory."

Her scruples and principles were still flying proudly,
she thought, but her willpower was nil. She looked
up at him.

His breath caught suddenly. "What is it?" he pleaded softly. "Tell me what's wrong!"

"You wouldn't understand," she told him sadly.

"Try me."

Fumbling mentally for words she didn't have, Tory unwillingly released a part of herself and wanted to cry out when she felt it emerge. Too soon. God, too soon. She hadn't meant to tell him this, but he was entitled to know. He had to know. Hadn't that been why she'd brought him in here to show him the paintings?

"I painted a man once," she heard that bruised part of herself reveal in a gritty voice.

Devon was very still. "So that's it. That's why you wanted me to see the paintings," he murmured, adding quietly, "Tell me about it."

"I painted him because I loved him," she said in the strange voice that was rusty with disuse. "And I *couldn't* paint him... because I loved him. Because I loved him, I saw him with a lover's eyes. And because I painted him, I saw him with an artist's eyes. He was suddenly... two men. I tried to paint what I felt, but I suddenly felt differently about him." She shook her head, trying to untangle the threads of hard-won knowledge.

Devon spoke slowly. "You loved him... *until* you painted him. Is that what you mean?"

Tory almost laughed in wry appreciation. How neatly he had condensed months of pain! But she didn't laugh; she nodded. "I should have known better," she mused tiredly. "I made up my mind long ago to paint honestly, and that's something I never compromise on. When I painted him, the . . . illusion of lover was gone."

Slowly, because he seemed to want—need—to understand, she tried to explain. "For most people, seeing others is like looking 'through a glass, darkly.' The glass is murky, unless and until enough knowledge is gained to see clearly."

"What you're saying," he said thoughtfully, "is that we see a distorted image of those we look at. We can't see them clearly until we know them well enough to see what's there."

She nodded. "Yes. But an artist—a good one—can somehow bypass that stage of learning. It's as if an inner eye opens out of the intense need to *see*. With each stage of the portrait, each brush stroke, the image becomes clearer. Until, finally, there's no illusion."

Very gently, Devon said, "Has it occurred to you that if there'd been no illusion, your honesty wouldn't have changed anything? That if there'd been no illusion, the lover and the artist would have seen the same man?"

"Yes," she said remotely. "It occurred to me. *After* I realized that I'd allowed an emotional judgment to cloud what I saw."

"Tory—"

"I let my feelings control me, Devon. I relied on them. I believed in them. And I was wrong—*wrong* to do that. It took the truth of the painting to show me just how much I'd let my feelings influence me."

Devon took a deep breath. "And what," he said neutrally, "does all this have to do with your painting me?"

For a moment, a split second, Tory felt cornered, trapped like a terrified wild thing. Then the moment passed. Her eyes held his steadily, and she could feel the vulnerability that he had to be seeing in her. "You know damned well what it has to do with you," she whispered nakedly.

"Tory . . ." His voice was unsteady.

She stepped back abruptly, unwilling to let him say or do anything irrevocable until he understood. Wrapping her voice in tight bindings of control, she said, "If I paint you, everything could change. And the thing is, I may have to paint you. I want you to understand that."

In a voice every bit as controlled as hers, he said, "I want *you* to understand something, Tory. I only know how to be one man: myself. There's no illusion."

Tory finally allowed her fear to see the light of day and reason. "But what if I've built an illusion myself? The way I did before . . ."

"You're stronger now," he said.

Stingingly aware that neither of them had yet said words of love to each other, she realized then that they wouldn't. Not then. Not yet. And she found herself wondering with an unfamiliar tenderness about this man who could accept the unspoken with no demands.

"I hope so," was all she said.

Very softly, Devon said, "Why don't you show me the last painting."

She looked at him for a moment, then sighed in resignation. "Why not. At least you'll see how brutally honest I am. It's over there." She nodded toward the corner and Jordan's painting.

Devon went to the crate, using the tools still in the room to pry it open. But before he slid the painting out, he looked at Tory with an odd hesitation. "Most women," he said slowly, "would have destroyed it."

"Not if they were artists. And not if it represented their best work," she said steadily. "That's the irony of it, really. It's the best thing I've ever done."

After a moment, Devon nodded, accepting that. He slid the painting from its crate and propped it against the wall on a low shelf, then stepped back to examine it.

Wholly a character study, there was nothing to detract attention from the man himself; the background was shadowy, obviously a room but undefined and lacking personality. But the man . . .

He was raven-haired and blue-eyed, tanned and fit. And he was a beautiful man. His features were classically perfect, his smile charming. But a closer inspection revealed the flaws that Tory's brush had captured so unerringly. Vanity was stamped in the set of his head, selfishness and cruelty in the curve of his lips. The blue eyes were empty, surface only with no beauty beneath the sheen. Arrogance bordering on insolence curved his lifted brow.

Quietly, Tory said, "I haven't touched it since we

split up. It's an honest painting, Devon. With the best will in the world, I couldn't make him as beautiful as I thought he was."

Devon turned to look at her, his eyes oddly bright. "I don't suppose he's anywhere around here?"

"No. He said he was going to Texas; I don't know where in Texas. Why?"

Taking a deep breath, Devon said flatly, "Because if I'm going to feel threatened by something, I'd rather I could punch it out."

Tory laughed in spite of herself, then sobered. "You shouldn't feel threatened by him, Devon. When I think of him at all, I think of him as a mistake. Nothing else."

"He hurt you."

"I hurt myself. I was in love with the idea of being in love, and I saw a man who didn't exist. It's over, Devon. I promise you that."

"Then paint me," he said softly.

She stared at him.

"I'm not afraid of what you'll see, Tory."

"*I'm* afraid," she said starkly.

"We both know you'll have to paint me sooner or later. You'll never be sure. *I'll* never be sure. We can't have that uncertainty standing between us."

"Not yet," she whispered pleadingly. "I can't paint you now."

Devon came to stand before her, framing her face in warm hands. "Why not now?" he asked gently.

Tory's heart caught in her throat, and she swallowed it painfully. She closed her eyes for a moment, words welling up from depths she'd never expected to reach, all the denials and confusion of this day and all the other days melting away.

"Because I love you," she said raggedly. "I love you, and I'm afraid of losing that. I'm afraid of losing you."

Chapter 9

DEVON PULLED HER instantly into his arms, holding her tightly. "I thought I'd never get you to say it," he breathed.

"I haven't heard *you* saying anything," she objected, feeling tearful again and wondering with some distant, laughing part of her mind if the dratted man had turned her into a watering pot.

"Sheer terror," he admitted on a shaky laugh. He drew back just far enough to look down at her. "Of course I love you, *zingara*—why else d'you think the proposal was for real?"

Accepting his handkerchief, Tory dried her eyes and said reasonably, "How should I know? You could've just wanted a place to rest your weary head."

"I have an apartment in D.C. and half-interest in a large farm in Virginia," he said calmly. "I'm also gifted with a father, a brother, a sister, and a lot of friends. It's not a place I want, sweetheart; it's you."

She looked up at him a little uncertainly, but every doubt dissolved when Devon abruptly and with deeply satisfying enthusiasm demonstrated just how badly he wanted her. Emerging from the embrace with the dizzying sensation of having narrowly escaped drowning, Tory wondered what on earth she'd been worried about. And then she remembered.

"Devon . . . about my painting you . . ."

"We'll take things one step at a time," he said immediately. "I'm a patient man; I can wait." He grinned at her. "And in the meantime, I'll just have to think up a proposal you won't be able to refuse."

"You did all right the last time," she murmured. "In fact, you did better than all right. You did perfect."

Devon hugged her. "I'm going to remind you that you said that," he said. "Later."

The steaks had dried up in the oven, of course, and the salad had wilted; they started the meal again from scratch. And they had fun. Whiskey was underfoot and in the way, stubbornly maintaining in the face of all disagreement that Devon's leg was a tree to be climbed. He also seemed fascinated by the oven and had to be restrained time and again from roasting himself in his curiosity.

As for his two human companions, they had faced the problem standing between them, and if not solved, it was at least understood and clearly seen by both.

They might have been lovers for years in their familiarity, and brand-new lovers in their fascination with each other.

So much had happened since they had boarded a jet for Bermuda and flown together in storm and darkness; they had finally reached an interlude of merely enjoying each other in every sense of the word. Love and laughter filled the house and brightened worsening fall weather.

"I should make you rake leaves," she told him sternly one day.

"I think the leaves add a nice touch; we should leave them be."

"You don't care one way or the other—you just don't want to rake them!"

"That's slander."

"Is it?"

"Yes. You're calling me lazy."

"I have endless admiration for your energy, believe me."

"I seem to recall your saying something similar this morning," he murmured.

"Uh-huh. Before *and* after you served me breakfast in bed."

Laughing, he said, "I had to wake you up somehow. You know, I really think I should invest in a set of jumper cables to get you started in the mornings."

"You're doing just fine with your native inventiveness," she said dryly.

"You approve of that, huh?"

"Well, so far, it's been ... interesting. To say the least."

"Is that what you were this morning? Interested? I was under the distinct impression I'd tangled with a wildcat."

"Turn a woman into a feline, you should expect to get scratched."

Devon choked on a laugh. "Sweetheart, I'm corrupting you! You keep saying things that seem to shock the hell out of you."

"My God," she said faintly, "you *are* corrupting me. If this goes on much longer, I won't be able to trust myself in public!"

"Not to worry; we'll build ourselves a new world and not shock anybody."

"That does not help. I'm being advised by a man wearing an earring."

Devon advanced purposefully. "That remark, my darling love, was unfair and unworthy of you. And I shall take great pleasure in punishing you suitably for it. I'll cage my wildcat yet!"

"Don't count on it!"

"Just let me find the thumbscrews."

"Devon!"

"No? Then I'll rely on my native inventiveness."

"Devon!"

Tory was slowly gaining insight into Devon's apparent contradictions of character, and that delighted her not only because she wanted to understand the man she loved, but also because she was gaining those insights as a woman rather than as an artist. It was not the resolute, absolute stripping away of layers that her logical artistic eye would have done, but rather a gentle and gradual perception woven out of conversation and observation.

His patience, she realized, was the result of both a child's stoicism under the strain of a stern father, and a man's dedication to a painstaking and demanding profession. The subtle ruthlessness was also, oddly enough, a result of those same traits; Devon had learned the hard way to fight for what he wanted—although his fight would never be a cruel one.

The humor and intensity that seemed to conflict were actually, she came to understand, perfectly in step with the man Devon was. He was a man who felt things deeply, but his very control usually hid those feelings. The intensity escaped occasionally through his remarkable eyes. But his humor was the outlet he most often employed, and that was understandable, since laughter had always been a substitute for strong emotions.

Tory understood that when she remembered, all at once, the morning they had met. Devon's amusing conversation had neatly drawn her attention away from what had been his very real disappointment in missing his brother's wedding. And she recalled other occasions when both she and Devon had reached hastily, as if with one mind, for humor because there was too much feeling to be entirely comfortable.

It made her ashamed, that realization, because she

had been too self-absorbed to understand that Devon's laughter, like her own, had channeled powerful emotions into a niche more easily approached.

It made her ashamed, and it caused her to reach out emotionally with an openness she had never known in herself. She was vulnerable, but so was he; she knew she could hurt him just as he could hurt her.

And so she encouraged the lightness and humor, seeing it now for what it really was. And if their mood or conversation drifted into a more serious vein, she encouraged that as well, realizing that they had, each for different—and similar—reasons, locked far too much of themselves inside.

She had done so because her painting had demanded an inner focus, a concentration every bit as exclusive as Devon's control. He had done so because as a child he'd been denied a father's support and understanding, and as a man he, too, had developed a concentration and single-mindedness for his work.

They were both unpracticed in reaching out emotionally—but they were getting better, she thought. And they were enjoying the time spent in learning.

"I think you've gained about ten pounds," Devon said judiciously.

"Surely you jest."

He laughed. "Don't look so horrified, love. You need to gain another ten pounds or so as far as I'm concerned."

"I think I'll skip lunch."

"You will not."

"Look, fella, you should know I don't like being ordered around."

"I'll make a note of it."

"Why do I get the feeling I'm being ignored?"

"If you were being ignored, love, you wouldn't have gained ten pounds. It wasn't *your* cooking that did it."

"So I never learned to cook. I had more important things to concentrate on."

"There's nothing more vitally important than starving to death."

"Very funny. I cooked last night."

"Is *that* what that was?"

"You're treading a very thin line, you know."

"And you're perfect, even if you can't cook."

"Guile will get you nowhere."

"What about charm?"

"Sorry."

"A pitiful stare?"

"Nope."

"If I apologize?"

"You're getting warm."

"If I abase myself?"

"On target."

"You're a tough lady."

"Devon? Why did you lift me up? And where are we going?"

"We're going to negotiate, my love."

"I'll never relent. *Never.*"

But, of course, she did.

* * *

Tory had fallen in love totally against her will, fighting and denying every step of the way. She had recognized her own feelings only gradually, and the fear of being hurt again had delayed the realization even more. But she knew how she felt now, and because she'd gotten to know Devon, she trusted those feelings as being real.

It had surprised her to discover that what she had felt for Jordan had been, as she'd told Devon, only a love of being in love. Inevitably comparing this time with Devon to the early days with Jordan, she saw finally, ruefully, that there *was* no comparison.

There had been silences between her and Jordan, long silences during which neither had found anything to say. He had laughed at her rather than with her, puzzled more often than not by the quick, dry humor she'd inherited from her father; his own wit had been sardonic and sharp—sharp enough to cut himself— but it was instinctively sly rather than thoughtful. With the conversational ball in his court, Jordan had all too often missed the shot. He had found nothing endearing in her reluctance to face the morning, expressing only impatience and irritation. There had been no understanding of her need to paint, but only a surface, selfish pride in the fact that she was "artistic."

His job in the glittering world of advertising had involved gimmicky slogans and glamorous parties where he'd used his charm to best effect. He had "worked" the room with her on his arm, always managing to mention her father's famous name and to heavily imply ties between himself and the art world.

God, what a fool she had been! In love with a beautiful face and a charming smile, hypnotized like some idiot adolescent with a hopeless crush!

But Devon...

There were few silences between them, and those were companionable and comfortable. He laughed with her constantly, responding with an instant understanding to her words and her mood. And Devon *never* missed a conversational ball. He teased her about her morning doldrums, her inability to cook more than the least complicated of dishes, and her occasional moodiness; and somehow, he always sparked her own sense of humor and made her feel good about herself.

He delighted in her unintended off-color remarks, clearly taking an enormous satisfaction in the freedom she felt to say what she liked to him—even if she was still vaguely horrified by her own unguarded tongue. He couldn't be in the same room without being near her, or near without touching her. And he held her in the night as though afraid of losing her.

Tory had very quickly discovered, partly through the continued existence of her fire-devil, that the only time Devon could hide no part of himself from her, the only time he truly lost control, was when they made love.

She was slower in realizing that she, too, bared her soul in his arms.

It was more than passion, more than desire. They would cling together, their murmured voices barely human, sharing the harrowing intimacy of gazing into each other's souls. No walls, no barriers, no shells to hide away in.

And with every night of sharing, the words became easier.

"Devon?"

"Hmm?"

"I love you."

"I'm glad, sweetheart. I love you, too."

"You were right, you know. We make magic."

"Mmm. Want to cast a few spells?"

"You're incorrigible."

"Insatiable."

"That, too."

"But you love me."

"But I love you. I can't think why."

"No?"

"No. Yes. Ancient eyes."

"Well—"

"And an earring."

"Tory."

"Sue me. I think it's cute."

"And will you explain to our children why their father wears an earring?"

"Of course."

"How?"

"I'll tell them that he's actually the reincarnation of a Scottish Gypsy—"

"And howls when the moon is full?"

"I'll tell them that when they're older."

"God help me."

"And then I'll tell them that their father seduced me with ancient eyes and blandishments. And an ear-

ring. That he flew me in a Lear jet along the edge of
the Bermuda Triangle. That he cooked breakfast for
me when he barely knew my name. That he conjured
up a storm and made the lights go out just so I'd tell
his fortune."

"I'll never live any of it down."

"Trust me; they'll love the story."

"They'll love their mother. They'll lock their father
up."

"Only when the moon is full, darling."

Devon was very still for a moment, then tightened
his arms around her as they lay in the lamplit bedroom.
"D'you know that's the first time you've called me
that?" he mused huskily.

"I like the sound of it," she whispered.

"So do I." He hesitated, then said slowly, "I know
we haven't really talked about it, and I know we're
taking one step at a time, but, Tory . . . d'you want
kids?"

"I . . . yes. Yes, I do. I always regretted not having
brothers and sisters."

He hugged her. "I want kids, too. Although I don't
know what kind of father I'd make."

"I know," she said whimsically. "You'd be the kind
of father who'd always cope with crises in just the
right way. You'd mend a broken doll or a toy airplane,
bandage a skinned knee, build a tree house. You'd
tell stories at bedtime and answer questions patiently
and help with science projects. You'd dry tears and
comfort broken hearts . . . and always be there when
they needed you."

Devon turned her face up and kissed her tenderly.

"Thank you," he whispered.

She smiled at him. "Don't thank me. That's just the kind of man you are, darling." And she knew then, beyond doubt, that Devon was indeed just that kind of man.

There were two people inside her—the woman and the artist—and the eyes of one didn't usually see things with the eyes of the other. But Tory realized in that moment that love, real love, had given her an insight equal to, if not surpassing, what she now recognized as her artistic intuition.

She suddenly had no doubts, no doubts at all, that if she were to paint Devon tonight or ten years from tonight, the result would be the same. It would be the portrait of a complex man with red hair and green Gypsy eyes. A man whose humor belied his intensity and whose control could be knocked into splinters by the love of a fire-devil.

A portrait of the man she loved.

"I always loved you," he said suddenly, hoarsely.

Tory looked at him questioningly, wondering at the intense certainty in his deep voice.

Devon stroked her cheek with fingers that weren't quite steady. "That first morning, when I looked at you, I knew I had to stay here. I didn't stop to ask myself why. You looked up at me with eyes that changed color and were wary, and I had to stay. There was something . . . fragile about you, something bruised and vulnerable. I wanted to hold you. All the time, I wanted to hold you.

"I had to be a part of your life from the very first

day. You . . . intrigued me. Your Gypsy eyes were gray and so solemn, but they turned blue when you laughed, and when I held you in my arms they were purple and mysterious . . . the way they are now."

Tory listened, still and silent and moved almost unbearably by the longing in his voice.

"I hurt when I saw those first paintings. They were so lonely, so bleak and beautiful. I looked at them, and I knew then how badly you'd been hurt. I wanted to find the man who'd torn those paintings out of you, and I wanted to break him apart with my bare hands." He drew a deep, shaken breath. "I'd never felt that strongly before."

"Devon . . ."

"And then the night you told our fortunes, the night you slept in my arms, I knew something was happening to me. You made me laugh even when I wanted you so badly that I ached with it. You smiled at me, and my heart"—he laughed suddenly, ruefully—"my heart went belly-up like a beached whale!"

In spite of herself, Tory giggled unsteadily.

He traced the curve of her lips with a tender finger. "That smile. You have Magda's smile, did you know that? Gentle, mysterious . . . as if you know something the rest of the world hasn't quite caught on to."

He smiled himself, the elusive quality Tory had so often seen and had never been able to put a name to lurking just beneath the surface. "And something you never quite caught on to yourself—mornings. Gray eyes solemn and puzzled, you wander around like a lost waif from another world. Every morning I want to—to give you something to hang on to, because I can't help being afraid you'll slip away from me.

"God, Tory, I'm so afraid of losing you," he said, suddenly ragged. "I wake up in the night because I'm afraid you've gone. I've spent my life looking for you, and now that I've found you . . ."

The sound of his voice was the raw sound of a saw biting into wood, and Tory couldn't bear it any longer. She rose up on an elbow until she was half lying across his chest, raining warm kisses on his face. "I love you," she said fiercely. "I love you with everything inside me!"

Devon swallowed hard, his arms holding her tightly. Teeth gritted to keep back the fear lodged in his throat, he said very steadily, "I can't lose you, *zingara*. Tell me I won't lose you."

"You won't lose me," she said unwaveringly.

Green eyes more brilliant than any emerald gazed up at her. "You haven't painted me," he reminded, control torn by jagged hope.

"I don't have to," she whispered.

"Tory, love, I want you to be sure. It'd kill me if it all fell apart one day—"

Her fingers touched his lips, cutting off the painful words. "Darling, I've loved only one other man in my life: my father. I didn't have to paint him to see what was there. I don't have to paint you."

Devon waited, still, holding his breath as her sensitive fingers traced each feature as though she were blind and saw only through touch.

"I see what's there," she said huskily. "What will

always be there. I see strength, humor, understanding. I see a man who makes me laugh, and cry, and sometimes hurt inside . . . because I love him so much. I see a man who brought me flowers, poetry, and a kitten. A man who looks at my paintings and sees what they cost me. A man who holds me when I feel lost.

"I see ancient eyes, Gypsy eyes, and they're branded in my soul." She kissed him softly but fiercely. "Devon, I see *you*. I see the man I love, and nothing will ever change that!"

Devon groaned deep in his throat, holding her as if he'd never let her go. "I love you," he breathed.

"Enough to marry me?" she asked shakily.

"I thought you'd never ask." He kissed her, desire laced with reverence, and Tory lost herself in the wonder of his touch.

"Why don't we stay awake and watch the sun come up," he murmured a long time later.

Tory's chuckle was muffled against his neck. "Suits me. As long as I don't have to *wake* up and watch it."

"Well, I'm all for skipping tomorrow, if you like. We'll just go on with tonight."

"That doesn't make sense," she observed thoughtfully.

"Sure it does. Think about it."

She did. "It doesn't make sense."

"So what d'you expect in the middle of the night?"

"Rationality."

"You can forget that. I'm barely sane, let alone rational."

"Why're you barely sane?"

"Love does that to me."

"'Lord, what fools these mortals be'?"

"Something like that."

"You can still back out of the wedding, you know."

"No way. In fact, love, I'm perfectly willing to wake up a preacher right now."

"We have to have blood tests and wait three days."

"I'll borrow Bobby's Lear again and fly us to Nevada."

"The anxious bridegroom."

"You betcha. I'm afraid you'll change your mind."

"Like you said, darling—no way."

"Caught at last, eh?"

"In spades. I'm a disgrace to women's lib."

"Does that bother you?" he asked politely.

"Not really. As long as they don't brand a scarlet letter on my blouse."

"Which letter?"

"W—you know, for wife."

"I wouldn't let them do that."

"My hero."

He was silent for a moment. "Tory?"

"Hmm?"

"Will you go with me on a dig next summer?"

"I'd love to, darling."

"It'll probably bore you to death," he warned carefully. "And the living conditions won't be a bed of roses."

"Well, you never promised me a rose—"

"Don't say it!"

She giggled. "Sorry, darling."

"You should be."

"My middle-of-the-night humor. Not top form, I'm afraid."

"I'll make allowances."

"That's big of you."

"I know."

She punched him weakly in the ribs. "You're a terrible man, and I don't know why I love you so much."

"Fate was smiling on me."

"You think so?"

"Definitely."

"Good. Fate was smiling on me, too."

"Then we agree. Fate was smiling on both of us. We, of course, had nothing to do with it."

"Nonsense. We helped. A little." She giggled as he swatted her lightly on the fanny. "All right, more than a little."

"A lot," he said firmly. "I'm not about to let fate take all the bows."

"Whatever you say, darling."

"I say it looks like the sun's coming up."

"It is, isn't it?"

"Mmm. I'll give it another hour or so before I call Bobby."

"Devon . . ."

"You'll be my wife before nightfall, wench."

"Darling, we have to sleep—"

"We'll sleep while the jet's being flown to Huntington."

"You're awfully sure he's going to lend it to you."

"My love, when Bobby hears why I need the jet, he'll not only fly to Huntington himself but will probably destroy airline schedules by pulling rank to get Phil and Angela on the next flight to Nevada."

"Good Lord," she said faintly, rising on an elbow to stare down at him.

Devon was smiling. "Are you game?"

Slowly, Tory matched his smile. "Vegas?"

"Vegas."

"Can we stop off at a casino on our way from the chapel?"

"You think we'll be lucky?"

"Darling, how could we miss? We're on a roll."

Chapter 10

DEVON SET THE cases down on the floor in the foyer, huffing mockingly as he looked over his shoulder at his wife. "What've you got in these things, *zingara*—rocks?"

"Yours may have rocks in them, since you packed them. Mine contain only clothes and a few pounds of sand." Tory shut the front door with her foot, setting down her case of supplies and equipment and carefully propping a canvas—hidden by draped cloth—against the wall.

"What *is* that?" Devon wanted to know, asking the same question for the tenth time at least.

And for the tenth time, Tory was evasive. "Oh, just something I filled time with while you were at the site."

Since she had shown him her various sketches of

the dig, the workmen, and the surrounding scenery each day, Devon was more than a little interested in finding out which subject she had committed to oil. But he had hardly wasted the months of their marriage in remaining in any way ignorant about his wife, so he bided his time. She would show him the painting when she was ready to and not before.

"All right," he said cheerfully. "I'll wait. And, for the record, I didn't bring rocks home in my cases. We dropped those off at the museum, remember?"

She came to slide her arms around his waist, smiling up at him. "I remember. You *would* insist on introducing me to the curator and then boring him silly with an account of your wife's artistic brilliance."

"Sue me. I'm proud of you."

"I never would have guessed."

Before he could respond, a feline howl shattered the peace and rudely attracted their attention. And before they could move, Whiskey had launched himself from the newel post at the bottom of the stairs and landed neatly on Devon's shoulder.

He winced. "I think he missed us."

Laughing, Tory reached up to remove the cat. "Remind me to thank Angela and Phil for keeping him for us—and for bringing him back up here."

"I'll also remind you to trim his claws," Devon said ruefully, massaging his shoulder.

Over Whiskey's loud purring, Tory said serenely, "His enthusiasm's part of his charm, darling." She stood on tiptoe to kiss his chin. "Like yours."

Smiling, Devon watched as she headed for the

kitchen to check on food and water for their pet. He bent to pick up the cases, nobly resisting an impulse to peek beneath the cloth hiding the mysterious painting before taking their bags upstairs.

By the time he came back down, Tory had thrown open the French doors to let the warm air in and reveal the late-summer scenery, and she was on the phone talking to Angela.

Allowing the side of the conversation he could hear to wash over him, Devon just stood and gazed at his wife. Like the artifacts he had devoted most of his life to, Tory's secrets had required long study and delicate handling to understand. And he had found her as fascinating as anything representing a culture long past.

Her tense fragility was gone now, replaced by serenity. Her Gypsy eyes were still changeable, mysterious, but no longer wary. And though she would never be a morning person, the months of their marriage had given her a sense of security that was reflected most strongly in the fact that her "lost" look was now a brief, fleeting thing.

He had seen her happy, passionate, angry, loving, puzzled, amused. He had seen her after a fall into a muddy river and after a horrendous trip by camel in desert heat. She had knelt beside him under the burning sun to stare in fascination at pottery shards, and stood laughing in a pouring rain that very nearly washed them away. He had seen her cope resolutely with insects and reptiles, easily with scientists and workmen, and cheerfully with students, half of whom had developed fierce crushes on her.

And he had watched as she sat on uncomfortable walls in ruins and on the shifting sands of dunes, her sketchpad on her knees and charcoal pencils in her teeth, behind her ear, and in her fingers as she worked furiously to catch some trick of expression on a workman's face or the last rays of a setting sun.

She slept on airplanes, on trains, or in cars, but never while traveling over water. She spoke flawless French and had a knack for picking up dialects. She loved horror novels and was perfectly capable of scaring herself half to death while reading one, yet she never hesitated to get up and go looking if she heard a strange noise at night.

He could clearly remember being shaken on finding her gone one night, only to discover her outside feeding a stray dog that had wandered into their camp.

She would, he had rapidly found out, make a pet of any creature that looked at her with sad eyes—and never mind that it could be dangerous. They had spent two weeks on the Serengeti Plain in Africa visiting a friend of his, and Tory and a *lion* had conceived an immediate fascination for each other. A wild lion. A big wild lion.

It was enough to give a husband nightmares.

And when Tory had requested at least a fleeting trip into the Sahara—"since we're in the neighborhood"—she had somehow managed to win the affection of the most obnoxious camel it had ever been Devon's misfortune to encounter; the creature despised him and followed Tory around like a puppy.

She had gotten a dandy sketch out of one incident during which that evil animal—she'd named him Spot—had cornered him in a tent. The sketch showed the creature's hindquarters protruding from the opening while Devon escaped through a nonexistent rear flap. And the sketch was captioned, in Tory's fine script: My Hero.

Some hero, he thought with amused disgust.

Unless she meant the camel . . .

Devon looked at her now as, entirely unconscious of his scrutiny, she laughed at something Angela had said, and he could still hardly believe she was his wife.

His Tory, his *zingara*.

Devon looked toward the wall opposite Magda's portrait, where Tory's painting of her father now hung. He studied the man whose blond hair was only lightly sprinkled with silver and whose brown eyes reflected the serene self-knowledge of his great-grandmother and his daughter, the man who had mirrored his bathroom because he never wanted to forget that he was, after all, only a man. And Devon sent a mental salute winging off to that man, for himself and for the daughter he had raised with such grace.

"Why're you staring at Daddy?"

Devon looked back at his wife, his Tory, finding that she had ended her conversation with Angela and now watched him quizzically. He smiled at her. "Just thanking him for the marvelous daughter he and your mother produced."

Tory sank down on one end of the couch. "You're

in one of your moods," she observed wisely.

"I don't have moods," he protested firmly, going around to sit down beside her.

"Oh, yes, you do! Like when you're staring at one of your relics. You know, long ago and far away."

"That isn't a mood; it's utter and complete fascination."

"If you say so."

"I do."

"I still think it's a mood, though."

"Stubborn. I have a stubborn wife."

"The pot's calling the kettle black. Besides, you're supposed to overlook my little faults."

"Oh?"

"Of course. I overlook yours, after all, and what's fair is fair."

"Zingara?"

"Yes, darling?"

"You're playing with fire here, you know that, don't you?"

"Are you going to turn me over your knee?" she asked, interested.

"Don't tempt me."

"I wouldn't dare." She smiled at him sunnily. "You could always send me to bed without supper."

"So you'd break your neck on the stairs sneaking down to rummage in the refrigerator during the night? And, speaking of which, shouldn't we make a trip to the store to stock the thing? I distinctly remember cleaning it out before we left."

"No problem. Angela stocked it for us this morning."

"I have a noble sister-in-law."

"I think so, too."

"How's she doing?"

"Mother and baby are doing great. A couple of months to go, and you'll have another niece or nephew." Tory laughed. "Angela's a bit impatient; she says she feels like a blimp."

"I can imagine," Devon said thoughtfully.

"I doubt it."

With a saintly air, he said, "Look, *I* didn't decide that women should have the babies."

"No, but I'll bet you think it's a dandy arrangement."

He considered for a moment. "Anatomically speaking, yes."

Tory giggled.

"I'm serious!" he scolded.

"I'm sure." Tory swallowed another giggle, then leaned over to trace a seductive finger down his cheek. "Darling . . ."

He looked at her warily. "Uh-huh?"

"You're not *too* tired, are you?"

Devon fought to hide a smile. "It all depends on what you're after."

"Well, we have all the makings for spaghetti, and since yours is so much better than mine . . ."

"You can't," he said, deadpan, "make spaghetti. Edible, that is."

"Exactly," she said instantly. "So maybe you could?"

"Maybe." He reached to lift her easily into his lap. "And just what'll you do for me in return?"

Tory linked her fingers together behind his neck.

"Anything," she said enticingly.

"How about the Dance of the Seven Veils?"

"I don't think I know that one."

"Improvise," he suggested gently.

She considered for a moment, then nodded decisively. "You got it."

"And I'm looking forward to it."

Laughing, Tory kissed him lightly and said, "Hold up your end of the deal first, pal. And while you're getting started in the kitchen, I'll go upstairs and see how much dust I can sift from our clothes."

Devon rose with her still in his arms, then set her gently on her feet. "You do that." He watched her disappear up the stairs, then headed into the kitchen to deal with spaghetti and a curious feline.

Less than ten minutes later, Tory erupted into the room with a delighted smile on her face. "How did you slip it into the case without my seeing?" she demanded without preamble. "*I* packed for us. And how did you keep me from seeing it when we went through customs?"

"The same way you kept me from seeing that painting." Devon laid aside the knife he'd been using to chop ingredients for the sauce and grinned at her. "I had a private word with the official."

Tory wrapped her arms around his waist, squeezing the comical-looking stuffed camel between them in her enthusiasm. "I love him, darling. Thank you." She giggled suddenly. I'm surprised you found a spotted one!"

"It wasn't easy, believe me," he said dryly, returning the embrace—and then some.

Her wonderful eyes glowed up at him with purple mystery. "I love you," she said softly, intensely. "And I'd love you even if you *didn't* give me presents."

"You mean I could have saved myself a few bucks?" he exclaimed in mock horror.

"Oh—fix your spaghetti!"

"Your spaghetti," he reminded her politely. "And that's what I was doing until a crazy lady burst into the room waving a camel at me."

Laughing, Tory blew him a kiss and returned to her unpacking.

Hours later, coming into their bedroom after his shower, Devon was riveted by the sight of his wife waiting patiently for him. There was nothing unusual in that, of course, except that she seemed to be in an unusually fey and sultry mood.

She lay back against banked pillows, the covers neatly folded down to reveal cream silk sheets he'd never seen before—and didn't really pay much attention to now. Because Tory was wearing one of his recent "presents," and she did things for that black silk and lace teddy that should have been, and probably were, against the law. It contrasted starkly with her smooth golden flesh and molded her slender body with a lovingly seductive hand.

Devon let out a long, low wolf whistle.

"Thank you," she said, solemn.

He cleared his throat and asked huskily, "Should I ask questions, or just accept a gift from the gods?"

"What you should really do," she murmured, "is deal with the champagne. I'm not very good with corks."

He noticed only then the bottle of champagne leaning in a silver ice bucket on the nightstand and the two goblets beside it. Slowly crossing the room, he sat on the edge of the bed and reached for the bottle, never taking his eyes off his wife. "The spaghetti was hardly worth this, love."

Tory smiled. "This is . . . in the nature of a celebration. It's been almost a year since that fateful morning you knocked on my door. And since we'll be in D.C. on the actual date, I thought we could celebrate a little early."

She reached for the goblets as the cork popped explosively, holding them while Devon poured the sparkling liquid. He replaced the bottle in its bucket, accepted a glass from her, and then lifted it in a salute.

"To you, *zingara*. To us."

The glasses clinked softly, and purple eyes melted into green ones as the wine was sipped. Tory obeyed the gently guiding hand at the nape of her neck, leaning forward slowly until she could feel as well as hear his whisper.

"I love you so much . . ."

His lips moved on hers tenderly, growing fierce with desire almost instantly. Her free hand slipped down over his chest, his lean stomach, finally touching the towel knotted at his hip, and she reluctantly forced her mind back to the surprise she had planned so carefully for tonight.

When his kisses trailed down her throat, she managed to say huskily, "I have a present for you."

"You certainly do," he breathed.

Tory set her glass on the nightstand, threading her fingers through his hair and gently forcing him to look at her. "I have a present for you," she repeated firmly.

Devon sighed, his green eyes still dark and passionate. "It'd better be good, wench," he growled.

"I'll, uh, let you be the judge of that."

He set his own glass on the nightstand, wondering at the diffidence in her face. She touched his cheek briefly before nodding toward a point over his shoulder.

"It's there."

Devon turned slowly, looking toward the corner. He had noticed nothing particular there when he'd come into the room; his entire attention had been fixed on her. But now he saw. The soft glow of a lamp on a small table lit her gift where it hung on the wall, and Devon wasn't even aware that he'd risen from the bed until he found himself standing before the painting she had so carefully guarded from his curiosity.

In the background was the stark beauty of ruins shadowed by an afternoon sun, their ancient tumbled walls mute testimony to old knowledge. In the foreground, the focus of the work, stood a man, his eyes narrowed against the red sun, his collar open to the faint breeze. He held a clay figurine in his hands, its surface cracked by time. But his attention was focused somewhere else, at what a viewer could only imagine.

Fascination was written on the man's face, intensity in his vivid green eyes. His strong mouth was curved with humor, sensuality, and an odd bemusement. There was an honest grace in his stance and knowledge in the strong hands holding the figurine.

And Tory's brush revealed other traits as well. Determination. Patience. Sensitivity. There was an elusive vulnerability in the lean face, and the intensity of his green eyes held a deep and abiding love.

"I remember that day," Devon said in a voice that seemed to come from deep inside of him. "I looked up, and you were standing there watching me."

"Yes." Tory waited, almost holding her breath.

Devon came slowly back to the bed, sinking down beside her. "Is that what you saw when you looked at me?" he asked thickly. "That—that—"

"That beautiful man," she whispered. "Holding time in his hands and gazing at me with so much love in his eyes. That's what I saw. It's what I always see. It's why I had to paint you."

Devon reached to take her hands, holding them in his own unsteady ones as he bent his head over them. Pressing soft kisses into her palms, he whispered, "Thank you, love. It's a priceless gift."

"I only painted what's there, Devon. Don't thank me for that."

He smiled at her, green eyes bright and full. "Then I'll thank you for a doubly rare and precious gift, love. I'll thank you for giving me the opportunity to see myself as you see me. And I'll thank you for loving what you see."

"Devon..."

"My beautiful love..."

National Bestselling Author
PAMELA MORSI

"I've read all her books and loved every word."
–Jude Deveraux

___*WILD OATS*___   0-515-11185-6/$4.99

The last person Cora Briggs expects to see at her door is a fine gentleman like Jedwin Sparrow. After all, her more "respectable" neighbors in Dead Dog, Oklahoma, won't have much to do with a divorcee. She's even more surprised when Jed tells her he's just looking to sow a few wild oats! But instead of getting angry, Cora decides to get even, and makes Jed a little proposition of her own...one that's sure to cause a stir in town–and starts an unexpected commotion in her heart as well.

___*GARTERS*___   0-515-10895-2/$4.99

Miss Esme Crabb knows sweet talk won't put food on the table–so she's bent on finding a sensible man to marry. Cleavis Rhy seems like a smart choice...so amidst the cracker barrels and jam jars in his general store, Esme makes her move. She doesn't realize that daring to set her sights on someone like Cleavis Rhy will turn the town–and her heart–upside down.

___*RUNABOUT*___   0-515-11305-0/$4.99

Tulsa May Bruder has given up on love. Her first and only suitor has broken her heart, and as the town wallflower, Tulsa figures she just wasn't cut out for romance. But when her friend Luther Briggs helps her to stand tall in front of the town gossips, Tulsa suddenly sees a face she's known forever in a whole new light...